BEAT IT OUT!

Dodger ace Magic Ramirez's pitch hit the edge of the catcher's oversized mitt and bounded away from Henderson toward the backstop. At third, DT Green saw his chance and grabbed it.

Racing toward home as fast as he could run, Green saw Henderson scoop up the ball. Ramirez charged in from the mound to cover home plate.

Green, Ramirez and the ball all reached the same spot at the same time. The collision was awesome. Both players went down in a heap.

As the dust cleared, the umpire could see David's foot lying across the plate. A foot away, Ramirez struggled to get up, the ball still cradled in his glove. In his judgement, there was only one call to make.

"SAFE!" Wendelson shrieked.

Other Books in the ROOKIES series:

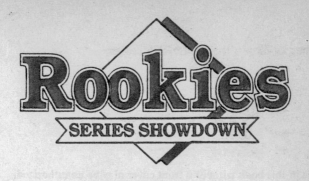

Mark Freeman

BALLANTINE BOOKS ● NEW YORK

RLI: <u>VL: 6 & up</u>
IL: 6 & up

Copyright © 1989 by Jeffrey Weiss Group, Inc.

Produced by Jeffrey Group, Inc.
96 Morton Street
New York, New York 10014

All rights reserved under International and Pan-American Copyright Conventions. Published in the United States of America by Ballantine Books, a division of Random House, Inc., New York, and simultaneously in Canada by Random House of Canada Limited, Toronto.

Library of Congress Catalog Card Number: 89-90968

ISBN 0-345-35907-0

Printed in Canada

First Edition: October 1989

16 15 14 13 12 11 10 9 8 7

Special thanks to Mark Crose.

To my editor, Paul Dinas. Thanks for all your
hard work, guidance, and assistance.

ONE

"Good afternoon, ladies and gentlemen, this is Brad Thomas . . ."

" . . .and Vince Perelli . . ."

" . . .welcoming you to historic Fenway Park, on a gorgeous, clear day, for the first game of the World Series between the hometown Boston Red Sox and the visiting Los Angeles Dodgers!"

The television announcer's voices rose in pitch to convey the excitement in the air.

"Vince, this year looks like a truly great match up."

"You're right about that, Brad. The Sox are loaded with power as everyone knows. From their number-one hitter all the way down to the ninth slot in the order . . . each and every one of them is capable of the long ball. Their team total of 230 home runs for the season is the most in club history."

"The late-season addition of rookie David 'DT' Green has proven to be a key factor in their success wouldn't you say?" Thomas asked his co-host.

"Absolutely . . . his clutch hitting and fielding in the last few games of the season as well as the League Championship series has helped in getting the Sox into the Series. He's been the main man the last month of the season, there's no question about it. Ten home runs and thirty RBI's since being called up — pretty impressive numbers."

"It'll be interesting to see how the young rookie responds now to the Series pressure."

Vince Perelli looked down at the volumes of notes in front of him.

"I talked to Manager Joe Morgan earlier and he told me that they're expecting great things from him. He's been absolutely unflappable since being inserted in the starting lineup for the injured Tony Ross."

The screen changed to the Boston clubhouse where the earlier interview with Morgan was taped. While off camera, the two announcers frantically rearranged their notes and wiped the perspiration from their foreheads.

Brad Thomas nodded in agreement with Morgan's closing statement as the camera refocused in on the two television announcers. "I'm sure the Boston fans are hoping young Green can come through like he has so far. But, on the other side of the field, despite all their power and hitting ability, the Sox are going to be facing a Los Angeles team with the tools to shut down their powerful scoring machine."

"Absolutely, Brad. There is a real contrast in styles. The Sox are ready to pound you into submission . . . the Dodgers will stop you with pitching and defense, scratching out a few runs here and there to win."

Thomas listened through his headphones to the television director's voice barking out instructions to him, while continuing to smile and appear to be listening to Perelli. Everyone in the broadcast booth was keyed up. It was important for the network to get off to a good start in their telecast and everyone was straining to do it right. He never missed a beat as his co-anchor finished his lead in.

"Led by two former Cy Young Award winners, plus an outstanding young rookie named Roberto Ramirez, the Dodger staff is loaded with talent. Ramirez came on after being called up from Albuquerque and did an outstanding job for his team. He wound up pitching the pennant clincher as well as two solid games in the League Championship Series. His ERA of 1.67 and average of 10.23 strikeouts per nine innings pitched are mind boggling. He should see considerable action during this series."

"That's right, Brad. It will be a true, old-fashioned test of pitching versus hitting in this series.

And, as you know, the Dodgers are no strangers to post-season play and it might be that extra experience that makes the difference."

"Tommy Lasorda spoke to us before the game, and shared his thoughts about that, Vince."

"An interesting story there. He's a very confident manager going into this important series. Of course, he's always built his teams around defense, pitching and speed . . . and that's what he's got this year. I'm sure he's happy with what they've accomplished so far."

While the taped film clip of the interview with Lasorda ran on the air, the director's voice echoed in both announcer's earphones, "After the tape there's thirty seconds till commercial break!"

When the red light of the camera in front of them flicked back on, Thomas and Perelli were ready.

"We're looking forward to a great Series," Thomas said.

Perelli jumped in, "The Los Angeles Dodgers, winners of ninety-six games this year . . . versus the Boston Red Sox, who won ninety-two times. It should be an exciting match-up. We'll be right back to introduce the players after these commercial messages."

The red light stayed on for several agonizing seconds as the two anchors smiled into the camera. When it finally flipped off, they both slumped in their chairs and sighed. The director called through the headphones, "Good work, men. Smooth so far . . . let's keep it up!"

Thomas and Perelli looked at each other and gave each other a high five.

"It's gonna be a good series," Perelli shouted.

Thomas nodded, "You know it, partner . . . you know it!"

David Green sat on the hard wooden bench in the Boston dugout pounding his fist into his glove. Excited, happy and strangely confident, he was anxious to get the show on the road. The team's pregame warm-ups were already over, and they were waiting for their cue from the television network for the introduction of players.

He had watched the Dodgers' warmup, searching for his friend, Magic. But since he wasn't scheduled to pitch today, Roberto had stayed in the locker room with some of the other Dodger hurlers, going over scouting reports.

Looking out over the field, David was amazed at how different it looked from the regular season. The grounds crew had double cross-cut the grass in the outfield to give it the appearance of a checkerboard.

There were multi-colored chalk designs of their respective emblems on the grass in front of each team's dugout. Red, white and blue bunting hung from the railings and walls all around the stadium.

Not to be outdone, the fans had brought hundreds of banners and posters urging their favorite player and team on to victory. The colorful displays were part humorous and part hostile toward the enemy but were all in good fun and added immensely to the spirit of the big event.

The bright sunny day with clear blue skies seemed like it was made for a baseball game, David thought. When, at long last, the Naval Academy Marching Band started high-stepping in from center field toward the infield, David knew it wouldn't be long till game time.

Then the public address announcer said, "Ladies and Gentlemen, please join in welcoming the visiting players from the Los Angeles Dodgers."

A few scattered boos were mixed in with the polite applause and cheers for the Dodgers. But when the announcer finished with the last player and coaches, the crowd noise started to rise in a deafening crescendo. The fans barely heard the announcer's words when he said, "And now . . . your Boston Red Sox!!!"

The crowd was standing screaming, clapping and stomping their feet. As each player's name was called in turn, he ran out from the dugout to a place on the first base foul line.

David's heart started to pound when he knew he was next. He was pleasantly surprised by the ovation he received.

"Playing center field and batting fourth . . . David Green!"

He jumped from his seat on the bench and ran
out on the field. The crowd was chanting, "DT . . .
DT . . . DT!"

In the short time he'd been with the Sox, he'd
managed to win the fans' hearts with his hustling, powerful play. Since the very beginning of
the game, baseball fans had always loved a winning team and complained about a loser. Nothing
had changed in the hundred years the game had
been played.

David greeted each of his fellow teammates
with high fives as they ran out from the dugout.
The team was psyched up by the tension of a
Series game and the wild enthusiasm of their
fans. When Morgan and the rest of the coaching
staff was finally introduced, the announcer asked
everyone in the stands to rise for the National
Anthem.

David turned to face the flagpole out in center
field. He quickly glanced over and caught Magic's
eye as the two of them faced in toward the field.

Magic winked at him. David smiled and gave a
quick nod, then turned his attention back to the
flag. When the Naval Academy band hit their last
note, the crowd roared in approval with the
umpire's traditional order to start the game:
"Play Ball!" Both teams returned to their dugouts until receiving the network's signal to take
the field. The Sox then charged out of the dugout
to their positions.

Since it was the first game of the Series, there were the usual dignitaries to introduce. National and American League officials, city and state politicians and finally, the Vice President of the United States. Stepping out from his special box seat, he made the ceremonial first throw of the game. Boston's catcher, Rick Waldman, caught the slightly erratic throw and handed the ball back to the Vice President as a souvenir. The crowd cheered and continued cheering while Roger Cowans, their ace starter, looked in for the sign for the first pitch of the game. When it split the middle of the plate for a called strike, Fenway Park erupted in joy.

"All right! . . . Wayda fire, big guy!" David called out from his spot in center. He knew that Cowans couldn't hear him. It was more a release of his own pent-up emotions.

He pounded his glove with his fist nervously as he paced around in a small circle. Whenever Cowans started his windup, David would crouch down with his hands on his knees and rock back and forth on the balls of his feet.

When the third straight pitch rifled over the plate for a called strike, David did a mini-leap into the air.

"Atta way! We've got these guys . . . they're not so tough!"

David knew that a good start was very important for his team's pitcher. Cowans was the type of hurler who got stronger as the game went on.

You could get to him early but your chances got worse the longer you waited. If the first couple of innings were good, he'd win it.

The next batter, expecting a first-pitch fastball, choked up on his bat and shortened his swing to get around on the fireballing Cowans. His bat made solid contact, sending the ball right at the shortstop for the second out.

"One more, big Rog . . . one more!" David yelled.

The tension and pressure of the World Series was starting to ease for David. The butterflies he felt in the locker room were starting to disappear. He had hoped that once he got involved in the game, it would be like any other.

When Cowans tried to slip a curve ball by the third Dodger batter, Ricky Salazar, David knew there was trouble.

At the crack of the bat, David took off running toward the gap between center and left field. He poured in everything he had, then made a final mad sprint for the ball. Just as he was about to leap and grab the sinking liner, he heard the voice of his left-field teammate.

"I've got it . . . I've got it!" Mark O'Meara cried out.

In a moment of hesitation, David stopped his dive and took his eyes off the ball.

"Geezuz, no," he gasped as his glance picked up his teammate's path. Swerving away as quickly as he could, David twisted his body in a frantic knot.

O'Meara's glance met David's and in the split second of actual eye contact they both knew what was about to happen. David stuck his glove up in the air and waited for the impact he knew was coming. His hip felt the blow first. Then their shoulders and knees made contact.

The two players went down in a twisted heap after the bone-jarring collision. The crowd grew deathly silent as neither player moved.

Roberto Ramirez leaped up from his spot on the Dodger bench and cried out, "Oh my God, no!"

He couldn't believe what was happening. Almost before the Series even started for his friend, it looked like it was over. As the Red Sox trainer and coaches raced out of the dugout and headed for the injured players, Roberto sank back down on the bench and fought back the tears forming in the corner of his eyes.

Not in the first game of the Series, DT, he thought. *Get up, Green!*

TWO

Joe Morgan knelt down beside the crumpled bodies of his left and center fielders. Trainer Mike Culp immediately went to work trying to assess the damages. The Boston manager was relieved when he saw them both start to stir.

"Hey . . . you guys okay?" he asked tentatively.

David tried to shake the cobwebs from his head. The impact had knocked him out and as he opened his eyes he was confused about where he was. Propping himself up on one elbow, he started to lift his upper body from the ground.

"Hang on there a second, kid," Culp told him. "Don't go jumping up until you get straight." Culp looked into his dilated eyes, suspecting a mild concussion.

Almost forgotten in the horrible collision was the baseball. But as David put his glove hand up to his head, the ball came rolling out of the web-

11

bing. He'd somehow made the catch and hung on
to the ball despite the impact.

O'Meara started rolling around on the ground
groaning. He reached down for his knee and grimaced in pain.

"Uhhhhhh . . . what happened?" he moaned.

Culp took O'Meara's leg and started slowly
stretching it out and flexing it. A sharp yell
stopped him.

Morgan looked at his trainer. "How bad?"

"Can't tell yet . . . could be ligaments . . .
maybe torn cartilage . . . if we're lucky it could
just be a bad sprain. He's done for today though,
that's for sure."

Morgan looked back at David, still stretched
out on his back on the grass. "How about you,
kid? That head clearing up at all yet?"

David tried to smile. "Yeah . . . get the car and
I'll be ready in a second."

Culp and Morgan looked at each other. Reach-
ing into his black bag, Culp pulled out an ammo-
nia capsule and broke it in two. He waved it
under David's nose.

Recoiling from the offensive smell, David
groaned and shook his head. After a couple of
seconds his eyes started to unglaze.

A stretcher arrived and two team members lifted their injured left fielder onto it. He was
strapped in and ready to be loaded when the am-
bulance slowly rolled to a stop on the outfield
grass.

From his vantage point in the Dodger dugout, Roberto Ramirez saw his friend David, with the help of his teammates, stand up and take a few tentative steps across the field. David hadn't figured out if anything was actually damaged yet.

"Take it slow, Green," Morgan told him.

"That's the only way I can take it Coach," David chuckled.

Morgan was relieved that his center fielder appeared to be functioning mentally again.

"Let's get him to the dugout and put some ice on all his bumps and bruises," Culp said.

"Ya think he'll be able to go back in?" Morgan asked him.

"I doubt it . . . but go ahead and get him in and I'll do a complete check on him. At least we've got our half of the first to figure it out before we have to make a decision."

"Good point . . . at least until the clean-up man comes up. That's Green!"

When the group broke up in the outfield and slowly headed for the dugout, the crowd rose and gave the two Red Sox warriors a standing ovation. With a teammate under each arm helping him walk, David contemplated doffing his cap to the crowd but thought better of it. He concentrated on getting in without falling on his face.

Culp immediately went to work on David when they reached the dugout. They checked over all of his aches and pains and determined there was nothing serious. The only question was the extent of the head injury. All during his examination, Culp bombarded his young patient with questions, making sure that David was mentally alert.

"Did either of you two call for the ball out there, Green?" Culp asked.

"Just at the last split second . . . I heard O'Meara call for it. I didn't even know he was in the area until then. It was just one of those things. We both came from so far away that neither expected the other one to get there."

Culp was pleased by the clarity David displayed in his answer. Shining a light in his eyes, Culp could see normal pupil dilation. He knew David was going to be all right. It was only a question of whether they should sit him out the rest of the game to make sure.

Jason Burke, the Sox lead-off hitter bounced out to shortstop to start the home half of the first. But when third baseman, Mark Lawrence, lined a single to center, the crowd started to stir.

David jumped up off the bench and headed for the bat rack.

"Whoa, there kid . . . we're not sure you're going in," Morgan called out.

"Hey . . . c'mon Coach . . . I'm fine," David claimed. "You can't keep me outta the first game of the Series!"

"It'd just be this game, Green. I don't think we should chance it. I'm sure if you rest today, you'll be fine tomorrow."

"I'm fine right now," David grumbled as he reached for a batting helmet. "There's no reason why I can't bat and prove it to you."

Morgan turned toward the trainer. "It's your call, Culp. He in any danger if he goes up there?"

"Probably not unless he gets hit in the head or something. His reflexes don't seem impaired at all."

David broke into a broad grin. "I'm ready." He slammed the helmet down and picked up his bat. He ran out to the on-deck circle before his coach could change his mind. The crowd let out a roar when they saw him emerge from the dugout. When the third Boston batter drew a base-on-balls, the fans rose to their feet as David dug in at the plate. They chanted, "DT . . . DT . . . DT!"

Roberto felt goosebumps run up and down his spine as his old high school buddy took his practice cuts. He knew the drama of the moment was something right down David's alley.

Roberto rose from the dugout bench and took a place on the first step to get a better view. He half expected his friend to look over for him. He didn't know when or how he'd do it, but he was sure that David would somehow acknowledge him.

When the first pitch from the Dodger starter, Val Fernandez, came streaking in low and away, the crowd cheered wildly. David stepped out of the box and slowly rolled his head around, stretching his neck. Culp took one step up out of the dugout toward the field, but David moved back into the batter's box before he could continue.

Fernandez checked the runners and then came in with a fastball on the inside corner of the plate. It was a pitch made to order for David, but he swung through the air with no contact.

"Striiike one!" the umpire screamed.

Morgan looked at Culp. "He should've had that one . . . you sure he's okay up there?"

Culp shrugged. "You tried to stop him didn't you? He wanted to go. . . . "

Morgan nodded.

David rose up to his full height in the box and then resumed his batting stance. He touched the outside corner of the plate with his bat, and swung several more times in an attempt to loosen up stiff muscles.

The Dodger pitcher tried to get him to go fishing on a bad ball, but failed. The count went to two balls and one strike.

"Blast it outta here, Green!" the fans yelled.

"One time! Just one time!" a fan screamed out, knowing he'd asked the same thing a million times and would ask it again a million more.

Fernandez's next pitch was a beauty. The fast-breaking curve ball completely handcuffed David, and all he could do was watch as it dropped over the center of the plate for a called strike.

Digging in a little harder now, David knew that he was in a hole. There wasn't a tougher

two-strike pitcher in baseball than Fernandez. He
had such an amazing arsenal of pitches to throw
at you, there was no way to anticipate the next
offering.

When David saw the pitch come down the center of the plate he knew there was something
wrong. Despite all of his instincts to swing, he
held up. When the ball made a crazy break down
and in on him, he was relieved he hadn't tried to
hit it. The ball bounced in the dirt in front of the
plate.

"Good eye, Green," his teammates hollered.
"Make him pitch to ya."

David leaned his head all the way back against
his back. He was still struggling with getting
comfortable, and his head was obviously giving
him trouble. Each little movement and twitch
made Morgan and Culp nervous.

Digging in hard with his cleats, David rocked
back on his heels and tried to make sure his
weight was evenly distributed. When Fernandez
went into his stretch, David's eyes focused in
hard on the ball, never leaving it during the jerky
delivery of the pitcher.

The pitch looked high and inside, but David
waited an extra split second. When he was sure
he'd picked up the ball's rotation, he started his
swing.

Making his adjustments in mid-stride, David
brought his bat around perfectly squarely into
the ball. The sweetness of the impact made it feel

like he was swinging through a vacuum: no resistance at all.

The ball took off like a roman candle. The fans out in the right field bleachers saw the ball coming over them before they heard the sound of the bat making contact.

In unison, the crowd leaped to their feet to cheer and watch the flight of the ball that was caused by this mammoth blow.

Roberto's head dropped down and he slowly shook it back and forth. "I knew it . . . I just knew it!" he muttered.

As the first two Boston runners rounded third and headed home, the entire Boston dugout went out to greet their slugging center fielder. Confetti filled the air as if the Series had just been won.

When David rounded third, he looked over into the Dodger dugout. His eyes met Roberto's. The two Rosemont high teammates smiled at each other. David pointed a finger and yelled through the crowd noise, "I'm waiting for you, Magic!"

"Yeah, waiting to strike out!"

When David hit home plate he was mobbed by teammates. They slapped him around and offered high fives everywhere. As he headed back toward the dugout, he suddenly dropped down on one knee. He righted himself immediately, but the slip was noticed by Morgan and Culp.

After the crowd and team settled down, Morgan went to his power-hitting rookie. "Nice job, Green!"

"Thanks, coach," David smiled.

"I think you've done enough for today, though. I'm yanking you." David's mouth dropped open. "You're kidding me?"

Culp joined the skipper and looked down at him. "We saw you drop down there after the homer. We don't want to take any chances."

"Aw, c'mon you guys . . . you can't do this to me!"

Morgan laughed. "Oh yes we can . . . and we are. You've given us a three run lead and a great defensive play. That's enough for one day. We want to make sure you're healthy and ready to go for the rest of the series."

David's head slumped down. He knew he wasn't going to win this argument. "Okay," he answered reluctantly.

Culp sat down beside David, and Morgan returned to his perch at the end of the dugout to watch the game.

Morgan's analysis proved correct. DT's three-run homer proved to be more than enough to win the game. The Dodgers couldn't get anything going against the Boston ace, Roger Cowans. A fluke home run in their half of the eighth only served to reduce the final margin to 5-1 in favor of the Sox.

As David joined his teammates in the clubhouse to celebrate their victory, he noticed that his muscles were starting to stiffen up. He told Culp and the trainer sent him to the whirlpool.

"You'd better come in early tomorrow and we'll give those aching muscles some ultra-sound if they're real sore. Be sure and get plenty of rest tonight too."

"I will," David assured him.

"And no wild partying . . . okay?"

David smiled. He'd been looking forward to getting together with his buddies, Magic and Glen, all day. "You've got it coach . . . nothing wild."

As he walked out the door into the cool night air, David smirked to himself. "Nothing wild . . . but a little celebration is definitely in order."

THREE

Glen Mitchell paced around the small press booth high above the field at Fenway Park. Soon after he returned home from his first season of pro ball with the Chicago White Sox, the editor of the local paper, the *Rosemont Register*, invited him to cover the World Series as a guest columnist. His official job was to watch all the Series action and report on games for the folks back home. But what the readers were especially interested in were his old Rosemont High School teammates, David Green and Roberto Ramirez. It was tougher than he thought it would be. Luckily, the column was short and the staff sports writer helped out.

When he finally left the stadium, he raced for the popular Boston restaurant, Yaz's. As he entered the crowded night spot, his eyes strained to pick out his friends. The place was nearly overflowing with people. Noise, laughter and music blasted through the air.

"Hey, Mitchell ... over here!" a voice called out from the side.

Glen spotted David waving and weaved his way through the tables to a booth along the wall.

"What's happening?" Glen yelled as he approached his buddies.

David and Roberto stood up, and, in the time honored Rosemont tradition, the three former teammates smashed forearms together.

"Good to see ya, Scrapper," Roberto said, using his nickname and throwing an arm around him.

"Great to see you clowns, too. Who'd have ever thought it'd be here in Boston ... for the *World Series* no less!"

David puffed out his chest and threw his head back. "What'd you expect, man ... isn't that what the game's all about?"

"Yeah, yeah, sit down and shut up," Glen barked, " ... before I reduce the swelling in your head with my fist!"

"Ooh ... sensitive, very sensitive," Magic teased. "I guess anyone could guess who's team didn't make it ... right?"

"Our team was too young," Glen rationalized. "We weren't ready for them yet. We haven't got enough guys who know how to win. We'll see how things go next year. We've got a couple of pitchers in the minors who ... "

"Enough," said David. "We were lucky this time around. Next year it could be the White Sox."

"That's for sure," Roberto nodded. "We might both be coming to visit Scraps next year."

"You better," Glen said. "I'm going through a lot just to be with you guys. It's been a pain so far."

"Hey, yeah . . . how's that going anyway? What's it like trying to write a sports column for the good old *Register*?" David asked.

"Today I just gave a bunch of comments to the regular writer and he's gonna work them into a story. After tomorrow's game, while we're flying back to L.A., I'm supposed to write my own story. Ya know, kinda setting the stage for what I think will happen out on the coast and how the Series is shaping up."

"That oughtta be good," David said. "You can explain how we're gonna wrap up the Series while we pound these guys into the dirt."

"Back off, man. You guys aren't gonna pound anyone, anywhere!" Roberto was offended. "You didn't exactly kill us today."

"5-1? . . . That wasn't good enough for you?"

"Take out your cheap three run shot and it's a 2-1 game and anything could have happened those last few innings."

David scoffed at his friend. "Yeah, right! And take away all five of our runs and you win 1-0. How's that?"

"Sounds good to me," Roberto shot back.

David rose up in his seat. "Well how about I play the whole game tomorrow and we score about three times as much as today? How about 15-1?"

"In your dreams, Green," Roberto yelled.

"My dreams are your nightmares . . . and yours are just beginning!"

Roberto's face started to flush.

Glen put his hands on his two friends' shoulders. ",Hey guys. Save it for the ball park."

Roberto and David looked at each other. The same thought was going through both of their minds. The tension between them eased.

"Glen? Glen 'Scrapper' Mitchell, is trying to break up a fight between us? Could this really be happening?" David asked.

"Yeah. We're used to pulling him off someone before he tears their head off," Roberto added.

"Geezuz . . . knock it off you knuckleheads. Or you will make me mad."

"Ooohhh! I'm shakin'!" Roberto whispered.

"C'mon . . . I didn't come here for this. Let's talk about something we can all agree on," Glen offered.

"Like food! Let's get something to eat. I'm starving!"

"Excellent!" Roberto pointed at David.

After giving their orders to the waitress, they settled back against the red leather upholstery of the booth. The restaurant was filled with memorabilia from Carl Yazstremski's career with the Boston Red Sox. It was the only team he ever played for in his twenty-plus year major-league career, so there were a lot of souvenirs.

Each of the former Rosemont Rockets was doing his own daydreaming as they looked around the interior of the restaurant. Roberto finally broke the silence.

"Ya know . . . baseball is a screwy game."

His friends looked at him with perplexed looks on their faces.

"No . . . listen to me. You've got Fenway Park . . . a natural spot for right-handed batters with that big wall sitting out there in left field. So you guys have a team loaded with left-handed hitters. You guys don't think that's screwy?"

"It is a little weird," Scrapper said.

"And how about the way they take the bat out of the pitcher's hand, when all through Little League, high school and college ball, the pitcher is usually one of your best hitters?"

"That's right, DT," Roberto jumped in. "Like I've suddenly forgotten how to hit after all these years?"

"Pitcher's usually aren't very smart I've heard."

"Maybe not," Roberto said, "but you don't find us pitchers insulting people like some dumb infielders do."

"Ouch . . . you got me," Glen laughed. "Please . . . if I ever come up to bat against you again . . . don't throw at me. Bounce a few at my feet maybe, but . . . "

"Hey . . . " David interrupted his buddies exchange, "look who's here!"

Glen and David peered around the room but didn't see anyone they knew.

David stood up and called out over the noise.

"Hey . . . Brogie!"

Frank Brogan, David's batting coach back at Pawtucket, spotted his former player and came to his table.

"Dave Green . . . how the heck are ya? That was quite a collision out there today . . . you gonna be okay?" he grumbled in his deep voice as he threw his arms around him.

"Geez, coach . . . you know I'm tougher than that. I'm gonna be fine. It's great to see ya again. You here for the Series I take it?"

Brogan looked at Glen and Roberto. "I taught this guy everything he knows."

David introduced his buddies to his old coach. "Roberto Ramirez and Glen Mitchell . . . this is Frank Brogan . . . the man who taught me how to hit, or should I say, lay off, the screwball. Without his help I'd still be in Pawtucket."

"Oh no you wouldn't," laughed Brogan. "If you hadn't figured it out by now you'd be on you're way home to start a new career."

Glen and Roberto shook hands with the burly coach and sat back down at the table. "We've heard a lot about you, Brogie," Glen said. "DT's told us a million times that you're the greatest."

"Thanks. But I can only take so much of this bull. I'm really glad to see you again DT. I'd love to stay and catch up with you, but I've got an important meeting I've gotta get to. Hey, knock 'em out of the stadium."

"You got it, coach!" David assured him.

Several other Boston players came forward as Brogan made his way from the table. Most of them had worked with Brogie their first year in professional ball, and they all wanted to say hello. David smiled as he watched him leave.

The waitress finally brought them their orders. David sat in front of a huge plate of barbecued ribs, Roberto stared down at a baked salmon, and Glen eyed a Porterhouse steak hungrily. "Eat hearty men, this is my treat," David said.

"Whoa! Why didn't you tell me earlier," said Glen. "I would've order this steak with lobster!"

Roberto smiled. "Why so generous?"

"Hey . . . wait till you see my order in L.A. . . . when you're buying."

"Maybe . . . I guess it depends on if we win or not."

"Bad attitude," David shot back as he bit into a rib.

"Now, don't tell me that you'd be buying if you guys had lost today. No way!"

"Nothing to do with it," David said.

"Yeah . . . I'll bet!" Glen scoffed.

"And that reminds me, Mitchell. When are you gonna spring for something since we won't be playing in your hometown?" David asked.

Glen nearly choked on a piece of meat. "Cruel, Green . . . very cruel. But nothing I wouldn't expect from you."

"Don't change the subject."

"I'm not. I'll tell you what I'll do. When the Series is over and we get back to Rosemont . . . I'll buy. That's my hometown anyway!"

David and Roberto nodded and immediately thought of their families. They hadn't been home for quite awhile, and Glen's comment brought that point back to them. They both missed their parents, brothers and sisters.

By their silence, Glen knew he'd touched a nerve. "Listen guys. Before I left town, I saw Coach Larusso. I think he's gonna try and make it out to L.A. for one of the games. He's really excited and proud of you."

"That'd be great if he could," Roberto nodded.

"Hey . . . ," David broke in, "that reminds me. When exactly are you gonna pitch, Magic."

"The opener at L.A. is what I've been told all along," said Magic.

"Hersfield going tomorrow?" asked David.

"You know it. Back to back Cy Young winners. Pretty impressive, huh? We were hoping to get a split here in Boston."

"If you don't . . . " David didn't finish the sentence.

"Yeah?" asked Roberto.

"Well . . . that's gonna leave it up to you in L.A. Major pressure for the Magic Man."

Roberto nodded. "Yeah. But on the other hand, if we pull off the win here tomorrow and I come back and shut you guys down, we'll be looking really good."

Glen laughed. "And if I get up every morning and drink a quart of milk for the next 960 months I'll live to be a hundred. You guys better quit talking and start eating."

"We'll see what happens soon enough," said David.

"That's right. I kinda hope it goes seven games and every one of them is a thriller right to the last out," said Glen. "I don't have to care which team wins. I only hope my two best friends don't fall on their faces and look like a couple of geeks."

Roberto looked at him. "Who you gonna be rooting for when he finally comes up against me?"

"I just told ya. Both of you."

"All right . . . stay on the fence. We understand."

"Feels good to me," Glen chuckled. "But, since Boston's in our league and I hate ugly pitchers from Chicago . . . "

Roberto and David threw the dinner rolls at him.

FOUR

Magic walked into the Dodger clubhouse deep inside Fenway Park. Running a little late since he wasn't scheduled to pitch, he was immediately swarmed over by a group of players as he entered the room. The questions came so fast and furiously that he couldn't understand what any of them were saying. It wasn't until Tommy Lasorda approached him that he started to figure it out.

"Ramirez," Henderson, the Dodger catcher called out, "how's the arm today?"

Magic felt his stomach tighten and his heart start beating faster. "Okay, why?"

"Hershfield broke his foot getting here."

"What!" Magic yelled. "You've got to be kidding!"

Henderson shook his head slowly. "I wish I was kid . . . you don't know how much I wish I was. First Salazar gets his finger smashed up, now

30

we've lost Hershfield . . . things are coming apart at the seams on us."

Magic sank down on the bench in front of his locker. "I guess I'm pitching today, right?"

"That's what the coach said."

Letting out a deep sigh, Roberto's eyes rolled up toward the ceiling. He thought about his family who'd planned to go to L.A. to watch him pitch the opener there. He remembered Glen telling him that Coach Larusso from Rosemont was thinking of going to L.A. They were all counting on him.

"Well, I'm psyched."

"Atta baby. Fire 'em in there, Magic Man. See you in five."

As Henderson walked away, Roberto reached up to his locker and pulled out his white and royal baseball undershirt. While getting dressed, he started thinking about pitching in a World Series game.

All those times I pretended to be pitching in the World Series while growing up," he mused, *". . .throwing rocks at tree trunks in the woods . . . hitting tin cans on the fence rail . . . breaking off curves with the whiffle balls . . . I can't believe this is really happening!* Pulling on his gray baseball pants and slipping his arm through the heavy, warp-knit jersey, Magic fought hard to control the wave of emotions flooding over him.

He thought about going to the phone and calling his family, but knew they'd be watching the game anyway and would find out soon enough. He realized it was more important for him to get out and warm-up properly before his start.

One by one, as his teammates finished dressing for the game, they filed by and wished Magic good luck.

"We're with ya, Magic!"

"Hang tough, kid!"

"You can do it, Rookie!"

Nodding his head, Magic acknowledged and thanked them for their support. The usually loud and boisterous locker room was strangely quiet. The Dodgers had been in plenty of big games before. And, it wasn't like Magic hadn't pitched important games for them already. But there was something about the World Series that made it all different.

Losing Hershfield for the series was weighing heavily on everyone's mind. Last year's Cy Young award winner and the Dodgers' ace with 25 wins during the regular season, they were counting on him for two or three appearances in the Series. Their chances at winning the World Championships seemed to be going down the drain.

Magic grabbed his glove and headed for the diamond. From the blackness of the concrete tunnel connecting the clubhouse to the field, Magic could see the blinding sunlight and the splash of colors that filled Fenway Park. He quickly made his way to the bullpen along the left-field foul line and started taking his warm-up tosses.

Wes Westrum stood silently, watching Roberto's motion carefully. He listened to the ball exploding into the catcher's glove. Leaving his spot next to the wall, Westrum walked up to Roberto and patted him on the shoulder.

"Looking good, Ramirez. You've got great stuff today."

"Thanks, coach." Roberto was surprised by the praise from his usually reserved pitching coach.

"I'm sure you can do it, kid. Keep us in there today . . . we really need this one."

Magic's head moved up and down. *Don't I know it*, he thought to himself and resumed pitching while he waited for the introduction of players and the start of the game.

The Dodgers led off the top of the first, so Roberto sat quietly at the end of the bench, desperately trying to control the battle of emotions raging inside of him. When L.A. was retired, three up and three down, he grabbed his glove and started the long stroll toward the mound.

Hopping over the chalk foul line, Roberto went straight for the rosin bag and positioned it carefully in its usual spot. He kicked the dirt away from the rubber and dug a good foot-hold for himself. Satisfied that everything was in order, he took his stretch and threw some warmup pitches to his battery mate, Steve Henderson.

"Whayda fire, Magic. Looking good out there," Henderson cried out through his catcher's mask to keep his rookie pitcher relaxed and comfort-able.

Magic grabbed the ball after his last practice toss and rubbed it tightly in his hands. He peered around at the crowd and adjusted his cap back on his head. Although Fenway Park was only about half the size of Dodger Stadium in terms of seat-ing capacity, it appeared to Magic as if the whole world was watching.

"Batter up!" the umpire hollered.

Jason Burke stepped into the box for Boston. The Red Sox dugout came alive with cheers of support.

"Get us started, Jason . . . get us started!"

"Be a hitter, guy!"

Roberto watched the Boston hitter fidget in the batter's box. He could tell that Burke was ner-vous. For some reason, that made him feel better.

"OKay..this is it," Magic said to himself.

Raring back with everything he had, Roberto let fly with his first pitch. In a last second desper-ate leap, Henderson grabbed the rising fastball before it went over the head of the umpire.

"Ball one," the umpire called.

Roberto shook his head and kicked at the ground.

Henderson fished the ball out of his glove, took a couple of steps toward the mound and fired it back to his pitcher. "Settle down, Magic. Don't overthrow. Just nice and smooth . . . okay?"

Roberto nodded. "Yeah right . . . nice and smooth." Embarrassed by the near wild pitch, he felt all 37,000 eyes bearing down on him.

"Stay within yourself, kid," Westrum yelled from the Dodger dugout. "You got a team to back you up."

His infielders behind him, echoed the support from the bench. "Fire it in there, Magic. You're not alone out here."

Magic tossed his head back and wiped his forehead. He waved his glove to his teammates, signifying that he was all right. He looked in for the sign and began his windup.

The crowd noise rose in anticipation as the pitch left his hand. Roberto grimaced as soon as it took off.

The Dodger catcher dropped to his knees and put his glove down, flat on the ground in front of him. When the ball skipped off the ground in front of the plate, he stretched fast to grab it before it bounced to the backstop.

"Ball two," waved the umpire.

Joe Morgan, the Boston manager, turned to his left and looked down the dugout saying to no one in particular, "I think the kid's rattled out there. He may not last long."

David shook his head. He wanted to say something to defend his friend but knew better. Instead, he sat silently and watched, but he knew Magic was going through a tough time.

When the third pitch of the inning again sailed high above the plate, Roberto looked over to his dugout. He half expected his manager to come out and jerk him from the game. But all he saw was a thumbs up sign and a smile.

Roberto went back to the rosin bag and tipped his fingers with the chalky, white powder. When he turned back to the plate, Henderson was lumbering out to talk to him.

"Hey, Ramirez," he called out, halfway between the mound and homeplate.

"Yeah."

Henderson reached his pitcher's side and patted him on the right arm with his mitt. "You much of a fisherman?"

Roberto looked at him strangely. "I've gone a few times . . . why?"

"How about after the Series you come out to my home in Wyoming and I show you what fly-fishing for rainbow trout is like?"

"Sounds good to me." Roberto waited for something else. But instead, Henderson turned and headed back to the plate. As he watched his catcher fidget with his equipment and squat back down, Roberto started to smile.

With nothing more than a simple comment about fishing, Henderson had broken the tension. Roberto suddenly realized there was more to life than this game, and it would go on, win or lose.

Roberto's fourth pitch was a blazing fastball. But this time it was absolutely, dead-center of the plate. Burke swung even though it was a 3 and 0 pitch. It looked so good. There just wasn't any way he could get any wood on the ball. It was by him before he got the bat off his back shoulder.

The next two pitches came in just as fast and just as accurately. Burke walked back to the dugout, not sure exactly what had happened.

"Wayda fire, Magic . . . atta baby . . . atta baby," his teammates screamed out. They'd seen him throw like that before and they definitely liked what they saw.

Lasorda gave him another thumbs up from the dugout and Roberto smiled back this time. Two more batters and two more strikeouts ended the scoreless first inning.

"Pretty impressive, kid," Lasorda smiled. "Keep firing and everything will be okay!"

"Thanks, coach. It was a little rocky out there for a few minutes."

"What did Henderson say to you? He ask ya to go fishing?"

Magic looked at his coach in wide-eyed amazement. "How'd you know?"

"Hey . . . who'd ya think taught him that? I'm not the manager for nothing ya know!"

Lasorda slapped his rookie pitcher on the shoulder and laughed. "Stick with me, kid. I'll get you through this thing . . . no sweat!"

The Dodgers immediately went to work on Boston's starter, Chip Reed. Waiting for good pitches from the junk-ball king, Corbin Reese worked a base-on-balls out of him. A stolen base and a single by Marty Barnett gave L.A. a quick run.

Reed settled down and retired the next three batters but the Dodgers were pumped up with their 1-0 lead. As they took the field for the second inning, the players hollered and clapped.

"Okay, guys. We're on our way," they yelled.

"Stuff 'em, Ramirez . . . stuff 'em!"

Roberto took the mound and looked down at the Red Sox lead-off hitter in the bottom of the second. He knew who it was going to be.

Pulling a bat out of the rack and jumping up from the dugout steps was David Green.

FIVE

When he worked up the nerve to look his friend David in the eye, Roberto was not surprised at what he saw — a big grin and eyes that radiated confidence and self-control.

Magic shook his head and mumbled to himself, "Doesn't anything bother that guy?"

Feeling his blood pumping hard through his body, Magic struggled to slow down his emotions. He knew he had to be in complete control to deal with Green's bat.

Roberto watched as David ripped a few practice swings and pounded the plate. He thought the former Rosemont Rocket had never looked as big as he did right then.

"C'mon, Magic . . . fire it right by that guy. He can't beat you," a teammate yelled.

"Yeah . . . right!" Roberto muttered to himself. "He can't beat me all right."

Roberto flung the ball into his glove and leaned in for the sign. It annoyed him that David had dug in at the plate like a camper setting up his tent. He decided he'd better do something about that.

I'll make him really reach for this one, Roberto thought. With a deep sigh, he started his windup and delivered the first pitch.

The pitch was fast and at Green's favorite height, but it was way outside. David make a split-second decision, moved his bat over then held back at the last second. The momentum of his reach pulled him off balance and he fell onto his left knee.

David calmly picked himself up, stepped back in the box and began his practice swings again. The crowd booed Ramirez.

L.A.'s catcher ran out to the mound. "You okay, kid?"

"I can't believe he fell," Roberto said. "I threw it too wide."

"Forget it. He has."

The two of them looked back at the cool and collected Red Sox slugger. "He's unbelievable all right," Magic said, shaking his head.

"He was hot in the LCS. Work him carefully . . . don't give him anything good," Henderson pleaded.

"Don't worry. He won't see anything worth taking a second look at. Let's just get him out of here."

"You said it," Henderson agreed as he trotted back to the plate.

Setting up on the outside corner of the plate, Henderson gave a big target with his glove and motioned to keep the pitch low. Roberto was in complete agreement.

The fastball was right on track this time. David watched it carefully. Roberto could tell that he was thinking about it, but he layed off. Just catching the corner, the umpire called it a strike.

"Whew," Roberto sighed.

Feeling a little better, he nodded when he saw the curve sign. The pitch broke down and caught the corner of the plate again for called strike two.

The fans were cheering on every pitch. They knew what this confrontation meant.

In control now, Roberto knew he didn't have to make any pitches anywhere near the center of the plate to get the strikeout. He'd just keep nibbling on the corners and hope to get lucky.

David let another ball go. When he got the ball returned from Henderson, Roberto went to the rosin bag and lightly dusted his fingers. He wanted to make sure he had a firm grip.

Roberto and his catcher hit upon the same plan at the same time. It was just like mental telepathy. A fastball, low and inside was what they both wanted.

The pitch felt great when it left his hand and Roberto waited anxiously for the outcome. He barely had time to get his glove up as the ball came ripping back up the middle, hot off the bat of DT Green. The ball was in center field before Roberto knew what happened.

David stood at first with a single. Magic knew his friend was waiting for him to look over at him. Sure enough, there stood his buddy, a couple of steps off the bag, with a huge grin on his face, giving him the thumbs up sign.

"Nice pitch, Magic," he said.

Magic didn't answer. Turning his attention back to the next Red Sox batter, Roberto really bore down. Three fastballs. Three strikes. One out.

The next batter wasn't doing any better, but on a 0 and 2 pitch, he lofted a pop foul that Henderson caught just behind the plate. Now there were two away with David still on first.

Working from the stretch, Roberto caught David out of the corner of his eye. He was sneaking a little too far off the bag, Roberto thought. In the blink of an eye, he whirled and pegged a throw to first trying to pick his friend off.

David had to spin and dive back to the bag but he made it just as the first baseman's swipe tag crashed into the side of his head.

"Safe!" the umpire called out, sweeping the air with his open palms.

David stood up and knocked the dirt off his uniform and rearranged his batting helmet. He shook his head to clear the cobwebs from the blow.

"Watch it, Green!" his first-base coach yelled at him. "He almost caught you leaning that time."

David nodded but continued to stare out at his former teammate. "He's not gonna get me . . . don't worry."

On the very next pitch, the Red Sox hitter, Dwight Evert, bounced a pitch right back to the mound. Roberto gloved it easily, but instead of flipping it to first for the third out, he spun around toward second.

The shortstop was over covering the bag, but Roberto held the ball and waited. David was chugging along toward second but knew he had no chance. He could see that Roberto was only playing with him.

By holding onto the ball, it forced David to keep running. When he was a few feet from the bag, Roberto then rifled the throw to his shortstop to get the force-out and end the inning.

David smiled at Magic as he crossed the infield and headed back to the dugout for his glove.

"What was all that about, Ramirez?" Westrum growled as Magic hit the steps. "The play was to first . . . or have you forgotten the fundamentals?"

"Uh, right, coach. Guess I was moving too fast."

"Personal feuds lose ball games, kid. Don't pull that stunt again."

"Right."

Roberto sat down quietly at the end of the
bench and tried to stay out of Westrum's way.
Nevertheless, he was pleased he'd managed to get
to DT in anyway he could.

The score stayed the same the next two innings. In the bottom of the fifth, Roberto went out
to the mound still protecting a one-run lead.

With only half of his concentration, Roberto
was able to make it through his warm-up tosses.
He watched as David stepped into the box to face
him for the second time. Henderson held his glove
and free hand down and patted the ground in
front of him. Roberto knew he was telling him to
settle down.

*I let him get to me last time. This time . . . I'm
coming right at him!* Roberto swore to himself.
The first pitch was just that. A bullet of a fastball
right down the center. It rose as it approached the
plate and David's vicious cut was well under-
neath the flight of the ball.

"Strike one!" the umpire bellowed out.

David smiled out at the mound as if to say,
"Give me your best!"

And that's what Roberto did. He came back
with his split-fingered fastball. David swung and
missed again, the ball breaking down and away
from him this time.

The crowd roared their approval.

David dug his cleats in a little deeper. He
cocked his bat back above his shoulder and focused his eyes directly on Roberto's.

He'll expect a waste pitch, Roberto figured.

Henderson set up on the extreme outside edge of the plate, calling for just that. But Roberto shook his head. He started his pitch for the outside corner but it moved just enough inside to catch the plate. Caught off guard, David only had time to flip his bat at the ball and catch a piece of it. It bounded down to third where it was swept up and fired to first for the first out.

"Wayda go, Magic . . . wayda fire!" his teammates hollered.

Magic kicked the rubber and pulled his hat brim down over his eyes. He reached for the rosin bag as he grumbled, "That lucky jerk. I should have fanned him!" The next two outs were a routine pop-up and a ground out, so going into the bottom of the fifth the score was still 1-0.

The mood in the Dodger dugout was upbeat. Although they were clinging to a meager one-run lead, they had that spark of confidence that made them certain they were going to win.

"A few more runs wouldn't hurt the cause gentlemen," Lasorda yelled at his players. "Why don't we try and get some insurance on our lead?"

But, in spite of their best intentions, the Dodger batters were having no luck against Boston's Chip Reed. The game continued to move along quickly in a low scoring struggle.

Before he knew it, Roberto was out on the mound in the eighth inning. It was time for another confrontation with DT.

Magic watched his friend stride confidently to the plate. He heard the calls coming from the Boston dugout.

"C'mon, DT . . . take this guy."

"Time for a dinger, Green!"

"We need one bad . . . now's the time!"

Roberto checked the position of his outfielders and took his stance on the rubber. Trying his best to ignore his friend, he concentrated on the signal and target that Henderson was giving him.

His teammates hollered out their own words of encouragement, but Magic didn't hear a thing. His concentration had risen to a higher level. The crowd noise, the cheers, and the jeers couldn't break through his wall of intensity. His eyes burned in on their target.

Roberto took his windup and fired the first pitch as hard as he could, challenging his former teammate.

David's swing was even faster.

His bat made contact and sent the ball screaming out of the ball park in the blink of an eye.

"Foul Ball!" the umpire's voice called out.

David's blast had twisted just right of the foul pole before leaving the field. The towering blast was nothing more than a long strike.

Roberto stepped off the mound for a minute and grabbed his rosin bag. Fingering it absent-mindedly, he was stunned that his best pitch could be hit so hard and so far. He was afraid of going back and throwing another.

Henderson trotted out to the mound to talk to his pitcher.

"What's the matter, kid?" he asked.

"What's the matter? Didn't you see that shot? Anything hit that far needs a ticket. Man . . . what am I supposed to do with him?"

"Just keep pitching, Magic. He's gonna get some and he's gonna miss some. That's all there is to do."

Magic slowly nodded his head. "I guess you're right."

"Just watch my targets. I'll keep him tied up in knots . . . trust me."

Magic rubbed the ball in his hands and smiled. "Okay . . . it's all up to you."

Henderson turned and headed back for the plate.

When Roberto looked down for the sign, he saw his catcher flash him two fingers then set up on the inside corner of the plate.

Inside curve? Is he crazy? DT will kill that pitch. Roberto shook off the sign.

Henderson gave it to him again and held out his hand in the shape of a fist.

"Okay . . . okay," Magic grumbled. "I'll give him what he wants."

The pitch came floating in and David swung. He was so far ahead of the ball though that all he could do was pull it foul into the right-field bleachers. The count was now 0 and 2.

Henderson set up on the inside corner again and signaled for a screwball. Magic saw the glove positioned just on the corner of the plate.

He let fly with his pitch and watched. David stood motionless as the ball headed inside on him. When it broke away and headed for the inside corner of the plate, it was too late for him to swing.

The umpire raised his hand in the air and punched out the call. "Strike three! You're outta there!"

Magic almost jumped off the mound. He pounded his fist into his glove and gave a thumbs up sign to Henderson. Roberto breezed through the last five batters. He'd done it. L.A. won by a final score of 1-0 and evened the series at one apiece.

The Dodgers were ecstatic in their locker room. They managed to get the split they needed in Boston and were now heading home to friendly Dodger Stadium.

Sitting in front of his locker and pulling off his sweat-soaked uniform, Roberto was all smiles.

"Congratulations, Ramirez," Westrum said as he walked by. "I knew you could do it!"

Henderson walked over and punched Roberto's shoulder. "Well, kid. Didn't I tell you I'd pull you through?"

"You're fantastic, there's no doubt about it."

"At least now you're gonna enjoy the post-game rehash with your buddies, right?"

Roberto couldn't wait to go find Mitchell. He smiled up at Henderson and said, "You better believe it. Thanks, Steve. A World Series win . . . I still can't believe it."

"Wait a minute, rookie," Henderson corrected him. "That was only one game. We haven't won the *Series* yet. Don't forget that."

Lasorda stepped in and interrupted their conversation. "Okay guys, listen up. The game went so fast tonight, we're getting outta here early. We've just got time to get back to the hotel and collect our stuff. We're flying outta here tonight instead of tomorrow morning. That way, we'll have all day tomorrow to rest up."

The locker room exploded with cheers and the team hustled into the showers.

Roberto grinned, thinking of his two friends. "And I don't even have a restaurant picked out yet."

"Say what?" Henderson said.

"Nothing. Time to get back home."

SIX

Glen Mitchell grabbed his bag out of the taxi's trunk and raced through Boston's airport terminal. Having overslept, he was afraid he'd missed his flight to Los Angeles. When he finally scrambled onto the plane and found his seat, he settled down and took a deep breath of relief.

"I made it," he said out loud. He rummaged through the pouch in front of him looking for a new tape to pop into his Walkman. He couldn't believe his ears when a familiar voice rose up from the back of the plane.

"Scrapper? Back here!"

Glen spun around and searched for his friend. Twelve rows back on the aisle he spotted him.

"DT! What the heck are you guys doing on this flight?"

David stood and walked up next to his former teammate. "Our charter got screwed up somehow. Something wrong with one of the engines or something, so we had to book a regular flight to get to L.A. in time."

"Great. Maybe we can change seats with someone and sit together."

David nodded and walked back toward his section of the plane. In a moment he was back, waving his friend to join him.

"There's a couple of extra seats back here. C'mon," David motioned.

Glen joined Boston's brightest new star and they immediately started talking about last night's game.

"Magic was awesome wasn't he?" Glen said.

"I'm glad he's not in our league . . . that's for sure," David moaned. "I'd hate to face him four or five times a year."

Glen whistled through his teeth to describe how the pitches looked from the press box instead of the batter's box. "Just a blur from where I was sitting," he said.

"Just a blur from where I was standing, too," David laughed. "I was lucky I got that hit off him in the second. Don't ever tell him, but I was worried."

"What about that shot you got off him that went foul? You hit that a ton!"

"I guess. I think the pitch was so fast, the ball just ricocheted off my bat that far."

"That's pretty unbelievable."

"He *throws* pretty unbelievably. He had me struck out in the fifth totally. I was just lucky to get a piece of that ball."

"Too bad we missed him last night. He must have been pumped after the game."

"Yeah, and I'd go broke paying to feed you guys again."

"I'm crying, man." Glen punched his friend in the shoulder.

David smiled and the two former Rosemont Rockets smashed forearms together from their seats.

"At least he's buying in L.A. — even though he's only playing one game."

Glen shook his head. "The way he's pitching? Lasorda'd be crazy to break his rhythm. He'll probably play every other game the rest of the series."

David looked at his friend for a second with a worried look on his face. After giving the comment serious thought he shrugged and said, "No way. He couldn't go that often."

Glen cracked up. "Hey, lighten up, Green. I was only kidding. The Series really has you spooked."

David stammered out a quick denial. "Naw. I knew you were kidding. Anyway . . . it doesn't matter. We're gonna get back on track and pound those dummies right into the ground. It won't matter what Roberto does. He can't win the whole Series himself."

Glen laughed. "Yeah, well . . . we'll see. But, boy . . . I wish we could have played just a little better against you guys. I'd have loved to have been in this thing."

"It's a kick . . . no doubt about it. You'll get your chance someday, Scraps. I'd bet on that."

Glen nodded his head silently. He turned and stared out the tiny porthole window of the aircraft to the lights below. "I hope you're right, man. I hope you're right."

David walked out onto the lush green grass of Dodger Stadium and shook his head. "I can't believe it!" he muttered over and over again.

His first visit to the National League city was an eye opener for the midwest boy. He'd been called up to the bigs after his last Triple A road trip to Anaheim to play the Angels, so it was his first time in L.A.

The hot October sunshine, the palm trees swaying gently in the breeze, the wild and wacky clothes and hairdos he saw . . . everything was bigger than life. L.A. seemed even more dramatic than what he'd seen on television or read in the papers.

Now that he was actually in Dodger Stadium, he still couldn't believe how incredibly beautiful it was. "Just look at that grass," he said to no one in particular. "Not a blade out of place."

Dwight Evert, another Boston outfielder, calmly explained. "Hey, kid. It's the weather. If Boston had warm sunshine like this year around we could grow a lawn like a carpet too. Forget about that. Let's go check out the wall and the warning track."

David enjoyed the sensation of sinking into the lush, soft turf as he trotted to the outfield with his teammate.

Evert had played in Dodger Stadium before. He'd started his career with Atlanta and had made many road trips to the coast. The sights and sounds of California no longer held any fascination for him. It was just another ball park to do his job in.

"C'mon, Rookie. I'll show you how to play them off this wall."

David watched as the veteran threw ball after ball against the wall to show the angles that they came off. When he was sure his pupil had learned everything, he came over and pointed toward the roof line of the stadium.

"I'm sure you know all this stuff by now, Green. Just make a mental note of the sun direction, light poles, wind direction, you know . . . "

"Gotch ya," David nodded. "Piece of cake. Let's get this show on the road."

After batting practice, the Boston team returned to their clubhouse for a brief meeting. Manager Joe Morgan went over the base-running signs for the game and defensive positioning for each of the Dodger hitters.

When cued by the television network, they headed for the dugout to wait for the introduction of players. "I hate this standing around," David said to Jason Burke.

"It's the worst, all right. It's the network, man. They've got us standing around like dummies waiting for their signals all the time. Let's just go out and play."

David agreed. "It drives me nuts."

The PA announcer came on just in time to interrupt the gripe session.

"It's about time," David groaned.

After the introduction of all the players from both teams and the USC Trojans Marching Band's rendition of the National Anthem, the Dodgers took the field.

Burke, the lead-off man for the Red Sox, patted his helmet down and headed out to the plate.

"Lead us off, man," David yelled out.

"Be a hitter up there," another teammate called out.

The crowd gave a polite round of applause as he stood up at the plate and then started to scream support to their pitcher.

The fate of the Dodgers in game three was in the hands of Terry Fulton. A crafty left-hander, Fulton had a tremendous arsenal of off-speed and junk pitches. It was hard for any batter to get a solid hit off of him.

Burke watched the first two pitches carefully, trying to get a feel for their speed and movement.

The first pitch was on the outside corner for a strike, the second one was low for a ball.

"Wayda watch 'em, Burke," his teammates yelled from the dugout.

After Roberto shut them down in their last game, the Sox were anxious to get their offense back in gear.

Fulton's third pitch was a roundhouse curve. Burke waited patiently for the sweeping pitch and timed his swing perfectly. He drilled the ball into left field for a single.

The Boston bench came alive instantly.

"Atta baby . . . atta baby. Here we go!" screamed manager Joe Morgan.

David jumped up and got his batting helmet on. As the clean up hitter for his team, he was now in the hole. "Keep it going now . . . keep it going," he yelled. Second baseman, Randy Bell, stepped into the batter's box. He looked down at the third base coach for the sign. When he turned to face Fulton, his bat was cocked and ready.

"Fire it by him," Fulton's teammates urged. "You got him!"

Obeying the sign he'd received from his coach, Bell slapped at the first pitch as Burke broke from first. L.A.'s shortstop moved to cover the bag for the runner coming down, and the ground ball bounded neatly through the hole created. Burke didn't hesitate rounding second and steamed into third just under the tag. The classic hit and run had worked perfectly.

The Boston dugout was going crazy. It was just the type of start they'd hoped for. Dwight Evert dropped his weighted practice bat and headed for the plate. David moved into the on-deck circle.

"We're rolling now, Dwight . . . keep it going!" David yelled to his teammate.

Unrattled, Fulton stood out on the mound and looked down at the Boston hitter. Working from the stretch, he floated three different speed-breaking balls up to the plate and got two over for strikes. He had Evert right where he wanted him.

David watched each pitch carefully, trying to get a feel for the velocity and movement. His practice swings were timed to coincide with Fulton's deliveries.

After watching patiently while two pitches just missed the outside corner, Evert knew the next throw would be in the strike zone. Picking up the rotation of the ball, he timed his swing and hit a frozen rope down the right-field line. Unfortunately, the Dodger's first baseman, Toby Harris, made a sensational leaping grab and speared the line drive just in the nick of time. He scrambled on his knees over to first to double off Bell.

The Dodger stadium crowd rose to their feet to cheer the outstanding play. A potential disaster had again been averted by the solid Dodger defense.

David slammed his bat down on the ground. "Damn . . . those guy's are so lucky," he cursed. But in his heart he knew it had been talent not luck that enabled them to put the play together. As he stepped in to face Fulton, David let his eyes roam around the huge ball park. *This really is some place to play ball,* he thought to himself. *A great place for a homer too.*

Pounding his helmet down, David shook himself back to readiness. The Sox still had a runner on third. Even though there were two outs, it was David's job to somehow get the run in and give his team that important lead. The book was out on DT. The Dodger pitchers were now well versed in how to pitch to him. Tight and careful. No easy pitches.

Fulton took his time out on the mound. Being a veteran, he was using every trick in the book. He knew a rookie would get impatient and he wanted every edge he could while facing Green.

When he finally nodded to his catcher, Fulton started his windup and threw. David watched the ball sail a good foot off the outside corner of the plate.

"Ball," humphed the umpire.

"Come on. Give me something I can swing at," moaned David.

Steve Henderson, the Dodger catcher heard his comment and sneered, "Don't count on it, rook!"

His remark made David all the more determined. If any pitch was anywhere close, he'd get some wood on it.

The next pitch certainly wasn't it. It bounced directly on the front edge of home plate and Henderson had to do a good job to prevent it from getting by him.

Burke danced off the bag at third but had to return when the Dodger catcher faked a throwdown. David motioned to him to stay put.

Fulton wasn't interested in throwing good pitches to David but he felt he should try and get something close enough for a possible swinging strike. He felt the outside corner of the plate was still the safest, so he aimed there again and brought his next pitch a little closer to the edge.

David's eyes lit up when he saw the throw. It wasn't anything to hit with power, but he knew he could move it. His swing was short, compact and extremely accurate.

Fulton grimaced as soon as he saw the impact. There was nothing he could do as the ball streaked over his head and zipped into center field for a single. Burke skipped in from third. The Red Sox had drawn first blood, 1-0.

Settling down, Fulton easily got the next batter and the first inning threat was over. All things considered, giving up only one run after his shaky start, he didn't feel too badly. The Dodger bench was enthusiastic in their support and vowed to strike back quickly.

In the bottom of the first, that's exactly what they did, mounting one of their famous hitless rallies: a walk, stolen base, a sacrifice and a fielder's choice produced the tying run. It was all they could get but, after one complete inning the score was even at 1-1.

Both starting pitchers settled into a groove after the first inning and for the next five, the score remained the same. This was exactly what the Dodgers had hoped for and Boston knew it. The mood on the Red Sox bench was getting increasingly anxious.

"We've gotta break out of this," Morgan told his troops as he paced the dugout. "I can't believe we only scored one run in the last six innings. *Nobody* can do that to us!"

Leading off the seventh for the Sox, Randy Bell was determined to get his team moving. Unable to hit any of Fulton's junk pitches, he waited for a big breaking ball, leaned forward and spun around just as the pitch reached the plate. The ball brushed his shoulder and he went down in a heap.

The umpire signaled for him to take first base. The Dodger bench came unglued.

"What're ya doing?" shouted Lasorda as he ran from the L.A. dugout. He got face to face with the home-plate umpire and yelled at the top of his lungs. "He didn't even try to get out of the way! . . . "

"Sit down, coach," the umpire growled. "I don't wanta hear it!"

Lasorda wouldn't let up. "You can't give him a base for being too damn slow!"

His pleas fell on deaf ears. His assistant coaches finally came out and pulled him back into the dugout. Nothing was going to change the umpire's decision.

David stood next to the plate laughing to himself as he watched. Lasorda was a great manager and knew how to use pressure. It just didn't work this time.

Evert popped out for the first out, and then David stepped into the box.

Connecting on the first pitch, David sent a shot down the right-field line, just inside first base, that headed for the corner of the outfield. By the time the right fielder, retrieved it and relayed it back to the infield, David stood on third and Bell had crossed the plate.

The very next pitch produced a long fly to center and David scampered home on the sacrifice fly. Four pitches . . . two runs and the Sox had a solid lead and held on to it to win the game.

When the Dodgers were finally retired in the ninth, Boston leaped for joy and they raced for the clubhouse to celebrate their important victory. Capturing the first game in Los Angeles was a big boost to the Red Sox. Angry they'd not swept their two home games in Boston, they were anxious to atone for that slip. Now, talk in the locker room returned to confidence in their ultimate victory.

"Good job, men," Morgan told his players. "We've had great pitching so far, and now . . . if our hitting's back, we're gonna be tough. You all played heads-up ball today and I'm proud of you. Let's do it again tomorrow."

"Two more to go, coach," someone yelled from the back of the spacious room.

"We're back in the groove now!"

"No problem!"

"Piece of cake," agreed David smiling.

SEVEN

A tennis ball came sailing through the air and knocked off his cap.

"What the . . .," Roberto said, looking around for joker with the good aim as he walked out of the player's entrance to Dodger Stadium. Suddenly, he recognized the familiar redhead with the deadeye arm.

"Scrapper!" he yelled after retrieving his hat. "Have a little respect for the losers, man."

"No pain, no gain, Ramirez. You just got to think quick."

"Yeah, yeah. I know. You see DT?"

"I figured you'd be out first. Nothing to celebrate about in your locker room. I figured you and me could go find Green together."

"Yeah . . . great," grumbled Roberto.

Glen lifted his forearm in the air.

Roberto's half-hearted attempt at a slam left nothing to doubt about his mood.

"Bummed out about the game, huh?" Glen asked.

"Yeah . . . we shouldn't be losing any at home if we wanta win this thing."

"Right on. That was a tough one to lose. Fulton pitched a great game. I think that deal with Bell upset him. He wouldn't have thrown a good pitch like that to David if he'd been thinking straight."

"History. Now we've gotta win the next two. It'd be a drag to split these two and have to go back to Boston for the finals."

Glen rolled his eyes. "Yeah, that'd be tough. Might as well lose tomorrow so you won't get jet lag."

"Stuff it, man. No way we'll lose three straight at home."

Glen slapped his buddy on the shoulder. "Hey, chill out. Got to keep your sense of humor. Let's go get Green, so you can buy us dinner."

"I can hardly wait," Roberto groaned. When they rounded the corner of the concrete hallway, they stopped in front of the players' entrance to the visiting team's locker room.

Glen flashed a press pass to the guard in front of the door and said, "Could you get somebody to ask David Green to come out for a minute?"

The guard nodded and stuck his head in the door for a second. After a minute wait, DT opened the door. Seeing his buddies he broke into a huge grin. "Hi, guys! Good to see ya!"

"Get your butt in gear and come on. Magic's got a dinner planned."

"Give me a minute to wipe off some of this *champagne*," David said, smiling. "Meet you at the entrance."

When he arrived at the main entrance, he had a mile-long grin on his face as he put his arm around Roberto. "Tough loss for you guys, huh?"

"Not as tough as yours the other night. We just play 'em one at a time, as the saying goes."

"Right," nodded David. "Let's see now . . . two more wins and we've got the World Series, right?"

Glen corrected his math. "And three more losses and you're just another trivia question."

"Funny, Scrapper. Very funny. Must be that column you're writing."

"Two games to one, men. That's where the Series stands. We'll see how things go when we get back to Boston . . . if we need to."

"You're gonna need to all right," argued Glen. "I've got this thing going seven games."

"No way," laughed David.

Silent during the last exchange, Roberto slapped both of this friends on the back with an open hand. "Save the predictions for the fans, men. Who's hungry?"

A moment of silence was broken when David laughed out loud and said, "As long as you're paying, I'm starving."

The three former Rosemont Rockets walked out of the stadium into the warm evening air of Los

Angeles. They found Roberto's car and climbed in.

"Hey, you guys," Glen said, fooling with the radio. "Guess who I saw in the stands today?"

Not waiting for an answer he went right on. "It was the jerk from East High . . . their pitcher . . . what was his name . . . Robinson or something?"

"Yeah, I heard he got into U.C.L.A. Man, that guy's a geek."

The conversation quickly turned back to high school days and the fun they had together. For the next few hours, the pressure of the World Series was forgotten.

Roberto walked into the dugout before game four of the Series, pumping up his teammates and offering his encouragement. He moved up and down the long wooden bench, nervously trying to work off the tension he felt. When he finally sat down and waited for the game to start, he was joined by his pitching coach, Dave Westrum.

"Great night for a game isn't it?" Westrum said as he peered out toward the skyline.

Not used to small talk from Westrum, Roberto just nodded in agreement, "Yeah."

Westrum worked the load of gum in the side of his mouth and casually asked, "How's your arm feeling today?"

Roberto shrugged, "Just fine."

"Not stiff or sore or anything?"

"Nope," said Roberto. "Feels just like normal to me."

"You mean," Westrum said, "considering you pitched three days ago?"

Magic was getting nervous. "I mean it feels fine, coach."

Westrum finally dropped his bomb shell. "Good enough to throw again tomorrow night?"

Roberto sat up straight and pushed his hat back off his head. He'd never thrown with just three days rest since turning pro. No one had ever let him.

Scratching his hair for minute, trying to stall for time while he thought, Roberto finally shrugged and said, "Sure. It feels as strong as ever."

Westrum patted him on the shoulder. "I'll warm you up tomorrow afternoon and we'll see how it goes. We've got Holland we can throw in if we have to."

Roberto started to get excited. "Naw . . . no problem. I'm ready to go . . . believe me. I want to pitch."

The full meaning of what just happened slowly sank into to Roberto. He realized that they thought a lot of him to come back to him in such a crucial contest. He was excited and happy as he watched the start of the game.

Boston jumped off to a strong start in game four that night. Jason Burke, the Sox lead-off hitter, walked then stole second. He scored on a single by Evert, and Evert scored on a double by none other than DT Green. When Mark Lawrence ripped a single to score Green, it was 3-0 Sox and no end in sight.

Lasorda went to the mound and pulled starter Danny Myers. He couldn't let the game get any further out of hand. Middle reliever, Eric Knox came in. He immediately got the next batter to line into a double play to end the inning.

The Dodgers came to the bench, dazed and wounded.

"Okay, guys," Lasorda exhorted them. "Gut check time! Have we got what it takes to fight our way back or not?"

"You know it, coach!" several players shouted.

"Then, let's see you do it!"

Shutout in the first, L.A. came back in the second to scratch out one run. The margin was down to two.

Knox did a good job in relief, keeping the Sox at bay, and in the fourth, the Dodgers broke out.

Corbin Reese beat out an infield single to start things off. Roberto edged forward on the bench sensing that something was up. The electricity in the dugout was on high and the energy was surging through everyone.

Mike Lambert came up, and after working the count to 3 and 2, fouled off four straight pitches. The crowd was going nuts. On his fifth try, he shot the ball through the hole between short and third for a clean single. Reese held at second.

"Okay, guy . . . you can do it," Roberto yelled to the team captain as he approached the plate.

Ron Feffer didn't wait long to prove it. Driving the first pitch with power down the right-field-line, the ball bounded off the wall. Both runners scored and Feffer wound up on second. The score was all tied up.

Toby Harris followed with the rarest of feats for an L.A. hitter. He took a 2 and 0 fastball for a ride out of Dodger Stadium for a home run. The fans were on their feet as Feffer hit home followed by Harris, giving the Dodgers a 5-3 lead.

"Let's go Dodgers . . . let's go!" The crowd cheered in unison, hoping to keep the rally going forever.

But Joe Morgan went to the mound and made a change for the Sox. He brought in their fireball-ing ace reliever, Tony Leonetti. He immediately doused the Dodgers flame by striking out the next three hitters.

As they took the field to start the top of the fifth, the Dodgers were greeted by an ovation from their loyal fans.

Knox pitched well for three more innings but in the top of the eighth, ran into trouble. As usual, it centered around David Green.

Pitching the powerhouse Boston rookie careful-ly, he wound up walking him to start the inning. Frankie Statler proceeded to double him home on the next pitch. When Mark Lawrence followed with a homer, the Dodger crowd grew deathly quiet. The Sox were back in front 6-5.

The Dodgers managed to escape the inning with no more damage. But, with Leonetti continuing to throw smoke in relief for the Sox, it looked bleak for L.A.

Retired in order in the bottom of the eighth, they took the field slowly, their heads hanging, to start the ninth.

Boston immediately pounced on the downcast National Leaguers and started off the inning with back-to-back singles. It looked like curtains for the home team.

Roberto sat on the Dodger bench, about to give up hope when he saw lightning strike. Boston's batter, Rick Waldman, smashed a shot toward third. Feffer speared it on one hop, right on the bag, turned and fired to second in the blink of an eye and the relay to first caught the slow-footed Boston catcher, Waldman.

Baseball's rarest event, a triple play, stunned the Sox and brought the Dodgers and their crowd, leaping to their feet.

"Unbelievable!" shouted Lasorda as his players returned to the bench. High fives were everywhere. The team was never more fired up.

"We can win this, guys . . . let's do it!" they shouted.

"Let's get two . . . c'mon!"

Charged by the turn of events, momentum was clearly on the side of the Dodgers. Henderson started off the bottom of the ninth with a double to the left-field wall and the stadium shook from the cheers.

Marshfield lined the very next pitch into center field for a single and the crowd rose to their feet. Henderson came steaming around third, heading home for the tying run.

But as quickly as the crowd had been brought back into the game by the triple play, David Green took it back out of them. Charging hard at the crack of the bat, he reached the single quickly, scooped it up bare-handed and gunned it home in one fluid motion. The throw came in like a fighter plane on an aircraft carrier — radar accurate.

"You're outta there!" the umpire screamed.

David threw his fist in the air and leaped into the air.

Momentarily stunned, the fans sank down in the seats. The organist started playing the theme from *Rocky* trying to pump everyone up. It took a while, but they started stomping their feet and clapping again.

Marshfield had kept his head in the game and went to second on the throw to the plate. At least he was still in scoring position with only one out.

His hustling play was rewarded when Frank West-phal hit a soft bleeder over the second baseman's head into right field. Again, the Dodger base runner round-ed third and headed home. This time there was no play. The Dodger bench leaped in the air. The score was tied again.

Leonetti struck out the next batter and the Dodger players were starting to think about extra innings.

When the count quickly went to 0 and 2 on the next batter, Randy Wells, the fans started to grow quiet.

Working from the stretch, Leonetti checked the runner and then burned in his fastball. Dodger Stadium suddenly became as quiet as a library. You could hear the collective sigh from the fans as they exhaled their breath.

Wells had managed to get around on Leonetti's heat. The ball shot off the bat and headed for left field. The Sox's Evert backpedaled fast and then bumped up against the fence. In a last ditch effort, he shot his glove up in the air and it came back down . . . empty!

"Home run! Randy did it!" his teammates screamed.

"We win! We win!"

Boston players started running off the field for the protection of their dugout. In a game of shocking turn arounds, it was fitting to end with yet another.

Roberto ran with the rest of his teammates down the corridor connecting the dugout with their clubhouse. The team was as charged up as he'd ever seen them.

The Series was now tied up, two games apiece. The Dodgers' fate would now rest with Roberto in game five.

EIGHT

"Have some more toast, Robbie. You're looking too skinny to me."

Roberto smiled across the breakfast table of his hotel's coffee shop at his mother. "It's great having you and dad here! I've sure missed you."

Rosa Ramirez patted her son's hand. "We've missed you too, Robbie. I'm so proud of you."

Carlos, Roberto's dad, nodded in agreement.

The Ramirez family had planned their trip to L.A. as soon as the Dodgers had clinched the NLCS. Positive that their son was going to pitch while there, they were stunned when he was chosen to pitch game two in Boston. They watched that game on television and cheered for Roberto, but now, seeing him in person was going to be something special.

Rosa continued to speak. "We read the box scores of the Dodgers every morning now. And thank God for television. We at least got to watch the play-off games you pitched."

"Well, today's the real thing. It's great you got to come out to watch me. After the second game, I didn't think I'd get another start here at home."

Rosa looked at her grown son longingly. The word "home" didn't seem like it should be used for this crazy California city. Rosemont was home as far as she was concerned.

"I'm kinda shocked the coach wants me to go again so soon," Roberto said.

"I think your manager is a very wise man," Carlos reasoned with obvious pride in his voice. "You've certainly been the team's most consistent performer the past few weeks. With Hershfield out, he needs even more help from you than before."

"I guess so," Roberto mumbled. His head went down as he pushed the food on his plate around with his fork.

"Robbie? Are you okay?"

"Yeah, sure mom. I'm fine."

"You're not acting fine."

Roberto pushed his plate away from him and leaned back in the booth. "You know it's hard for me to eat before I pitch. I never have much of an appetite."

"I understand," Carlos said. "Rosa . . . it's nothing. Don't worry. I'm sure after the game tonight he'll more than make up for it. Right, son?"

"My stomach gets tied up in a big knot. I'm fine once the game starts. It's the waiting. I thought I'd outgrow it. But I guess I never will."

"Would it be better if we didn't talk about the game?" Rosa asked.

"Oh no, . . . it doesn't matter. It's all I can think about anyway, so no big deal. We can talk about it."

An uncomfortable silence fell over the table though. Nobody knew what to say.

Roberto picked up on his parents hesitation and started laughing. "What's new and exciting in Rosemont?"

Everyone laughed. "Well, since you asked," Rosa began, "let me tell you what's happened to my apple tree in the backyard."

Roberto relaxed and lost himself in his mother's stories. He was glad they made it to L.A. and thankful he'd have them in the stands cheering tonight in game five against the Sox. It would be the most important game he ever pitched in.

Roberto warmed up in relative solitude out in the Dodger bullpen before the game. His regular catcher, Steve Henderson, worked with him. After four games of the series, there weren't any real surprises to go over in the Boston batting order. The scouting, coaching and talking were done. Now it was time to play.

When it was finally time to take the mound, Roberto sprinted out to the pitcher's rubber and

dug his footholds in their usual place. The rosin
bag was in its spot, the toe-hold felt good, and
everyone behind him in the field was in proper
position.

"Okay," Roberto said out loud. "Let's do it!"

Jason Burke stepped into the box to lead off the
Red Sox lineup. Roberto focused in on Henderson's sign. The crowd waited in anticipation of
the first pitch, ready to cheer their starting pitcher on.

Roberto delivered a fastball to start things off.

Burke rapped it into left field for a single. Surprised, Roberto kicked the ground and cursed
himself for throwing such a good pitch to start off.
He'd just assumed that burke wouldn't take the
first throw.

"No problem," Henderson yelled out to his battery mate.

"Let's take two," captain Ron Feffer called out
to the rest of the infield. He held up two fingers
and made sure everyone made eye contact with
him.

Roberto put one foot on the rubber and leaned
forward to get the sign. Working from the stretch,
he checked on Burke several times before finally
throwing over to first.

He's straying a little too far off that bag, Roberto thought to himself. *I'd better keep him leaning
toward first.* The cat and mouse game began.
Burke would edge his way as far as possible from
the bag. Roberto would go into the stretch, pause

and then throw to Toby Harris, his first baseman, to keep Burke from stealing.

Randy Bell, Boston's second hitter, stepped in and out of the batter's box. If Roberto held the ball too long, he'd simply raise his hand and step out. This sequence went on for over three minutes with no pitch going to the plate. The crowd and the players in the field started getting restless.

"Let's get the batter, Magic," yelled Westphal, the shortstop. "Forget about first base. He's staying put."

Finally, Roberto came into the plate with his second pitch. Bell liked what he saw and drove it hard down the right-field line for a single. Burke didn't break stride as he rounded second and steamed into third easily.

Henderson came running out to the mound. He knew he'd better settle Roberto down quickly or it could be an early shower for the rookie pitcher.

"Hey, Magic Man. Let's talk."

Roberto shook his head. "Fishing sounds great to me right now. What else have you got in mind?"

Henderson laughed. "At least you've still got a sense of humor. Listen . . . both of those pitches were a little bit up. I think you've gotta bend your back a little more and flex the knees. You're a little too stiff and upright."

Roberto thought about the advice. "Maybe you're right."

"Of course I am. No way those two guys could hit you if you're throwing the way you should be. C'mon . . . loosen up a little."

"Okay . . . I'll give it a try."

Henderson started walking back but turned around. "And don't try to aim the ball. Just throw it. Remember what got you here."

Roberto glanced up behind the Dodgers dugout. He knew his parents' seats were somewhere up from there but he wasn't exactly sure where. He could only look for a second before he had to turn back to the game. He couldn't see them in the glare of the lights.

Dwight Evert dug in at the plate to face him. Roberto knew that David was next. If things were bad now, they were only going to get worse if something didn't happen quickly.

"Blast it by him, Magic," Feffer yelled from his position at third. "You can do it!"

The whole infield started cheering their pitcher on. The crowd got into it immediately. Calls to, "Strike 'em out . . . Fan him . . . Go for the K!" could be heard everywhere.

Inspired by the support, Roberto reached down inside himself for something extra. Keeping in mind Henderson's advice, he let all of his energy flow naturally through his arm. The ball streaked toward home and was by Evert in a flash.

"Strike one," the umpire announced. Roberto came back with the heat again. The umpire's right hand punched the air again. "Strike two!"

Evert was on the ropes. The Boston batter had edged as far back as he could go in the box. He was choked way up on the bat. He was doing everything he could to give himself time to make contact.

Roberto knew what pitch he wanted to throw. Henderson gave him the sign and Magic smiled.

The windup, delivery and arm motion looked the same as the first two pitches. But this time it was the change up.

Evert's swing was almost completed before the ball even got to the plate. Roberto had his first K and the string of hits was broken.

"Whew," Magic sighed. "One down . . . two to go."

There were still runners on first and third though. And worst of all, DT was coming to bat. *I've gotta find a way around him,* Magic reasoned. *I can't let him beat us with one swing of the bat.* With the runners on the corners, numerous opportunities were available to the Red Sox. Double steal, hit and run, sacrifice, suicide squeeze — all of these options could produce a run.

But David was definitely thinking about one swing of the bat giving Boston a 3-0 lead. And Joe Morgan wasn't going to take that option away from his rookie hitter. His signal from the bench out to his third-base coach was for everyone to play it straight and wait and see what David did with the bat.

Roberto took several deep breaths while he waited for the sign from Henderson. Part of him wanted to challenge David, but part of him wanted to walk him and face the next batter.

Henderson called for the fastball, but set up on the extreme outside edge of the plate.

"Okay," Roberto groaned. "Here goes nothing."

The pitch was a good one: hard and fast, right for the target Henderson had given him.

Knowing he wasn't going to be looking at anything too good. David decided to go for it.

His bat whipped around and caught the ball out on the corner. The power in his swing made the ball jump back off the wooden bat quickly, like a rubber ball off of concrete.

Roberto whirled around to watch the flight of the ball as it headed for straight away center field. A wave of nausea swept over him.

Dodger Ricky Salazar jumped at the crack of the bat and started running toward the wall. Roberto tried to figure the angle of the flight of the ball and the path of his center fielder. To him, it looked bad.

Burke started trotting slowly in from third, positive the ball was out of the park. Bell was almost at second base. David still held onto his bat as he trotted toward first, waiting to see the outcome of his blast.

Just when it looked like it was over, Salazar reached the wall and made a tremendous leap. He got his glove up to the top of ten foot wall and speared the ball in a miraculous catch. Crashing back to the ground, he held on to what should have been a sure home run. David threw his bat down in disgust and veered off toward the dugout. Bell, slammed on the brakes and ran back toward first to avoid getting doubled off.

Burke, playing it halfway down the line, went back to third and tagged up. Before Salazar could stand and relay the ball into the infield, Boston had their first run as Burke crossed the plate before the throw.

A mixture of disgust and relief filled Roberto. He was mad that he'd let DT hit one so hard, but glad it hadn't gone out for a three-run homer. Now there were two outs and only a runner on first.

When Roberto got Frankie Statler to pop-out to short, the inning was over with minimal damage. The score was 1-0 Red Sox, but everyone knew, it could have been a lot worse. The Dodgers were relieved when they reached their dugout.

"Boy . . . that was close," sighed Ron Feffer. "We dodged a bullet there. Let's take advantage of it you guys!"

The rest of the Dodgers cheered in agreement. What could have been a disaster was now turning into a reason for their own rally.

Roberto sat silently at the end of the bench, concerned about his own performance. He wondered if he had what it took to win this important game.

He watched as the Dodger lead-off man drew a base on balls. When Marshfield followed with a single, Roberto was one of the first players on the top step of the dugout cheering.

"Wayda go, Marshie . . . atta way!"

The whole bench had expected a sacrifice, so the single was a big surprise to everyone. Lasorda was obviously going for something big right off the bat.

Steve Henderson stepped into the box. One of the only power hitters on the Dodger team, Henderson was ready when he pounded his bat on the plate and took his stance.

Tom Sneed, the Boston starter, worked Henderson carefully. Pitching from the stretch, he kept one eye on the runners and one on the plate. When he finally fired his first pitch to Henderson, it came in high and tight.

Wheeling fast to clear out of the path of the ball, Henderson fell to the ground. He jumped up and took a step toward the mound, but quickly settled down. He realized now was not the time to lose his temper. The Dodger's dugout blasted Sneed with whistles, jeers and cat calls.

"C'mon Stever . . . blast him!"

"Rip one right through him," they yelled.

"All the way . . . be a hero!"

Roberto watched as the next pitch came in. Henderson, keyed up from the last throw, jumped all over it. In his haste, he slightly over swung. He made contact, but it wasn't as pure as it could have been. The ball flew toward the wall, but just didn't have enough to make it.

It hit the wall and bounded back toward the infield as the runners raced around the bases.

O'Meara, the Red Sox left fielder, chased down the elusive ball and rifled it into second. Off at the crack of the bat, Marshfield legged it all the way home from first, just beating the relay and tag. Henderson, trying to stretch the sure double into a possible triple, failed. The throw down to third nailed him for the first out. But the Dodgers were now on top, 2-1.

Sneed settled down and got the next two batters to end the first inning. It had been a wild one, and the crowd roared its approval.

Roberto walked slowly to the mound to start the second. He was working hard to gain his composure. The rocky start in the first was weighing heavily on his mind. The pressure was definitely getting to him.

There really was no tomorrow for his team. A loss today would send them back to Boston down three games to two. A situation that no team would like to try and overcome.

Trying to pump himself up, Roberto kicked at the ground as he walked and tried to fight back the knots forming in his muscles. The tension was robbing him of his control.

His ears suddenly picked up as he approached the rubber. He thought he heard a familiar voice rise above the din of the crowd. "You can do it, Robbie!"

A smile creased Roberto's face. *That sure sounds like mom,* he thought.

His mind flooded with memories of his high school days, when her encouragement had many times carried him through tough times. As he took his warm-up tosses, Roberto started to feel better. Henderson noticed there was a return to form in his pitcher. The graceful, fluid motion of Roberto's delivery was back. The ball was popping into his glove with tremendous speed and power. After the nine warm-up tosses and a throw down to second, the Dodger catcher gave Roberto the high sign.

Pacing around on his little raised circle of dirt, Roberto waited for the first batter to step in. The fire was burning brightly in his eyes again. He slapped his thigh with his glove hand and reached for the rosin bag.

The Dodger infielders started their chatter, trying to inspire their pitcher.

"Looking good out there," Henderson yelled out from behind the plate.

Magic smiled and nodded. He knew it. Suddenly, the tension drained from him. The magic was back.

NINE

Roberto breezed through the second inning, retiring the side on seven pitches. It was as if the first inning hadn't happened. His pitches had zip and zing on them, dancing every which way as they crossed the plate.

David sat in the Boston dugout shaking his head. He wanted to find his teammate who suggested that they might be able to "knock the kid out early" and tell him off. David had seen it all before and knew what was in store for his team.

Grabbing his glove and racing out on the field, he realized it was going to take something very special to beat his friend today. They were going to be lucky to get to him again.

It was a mixture of pride and anxiety that clouded his judgement. On the one hand, he was happy for Roberto. But on the other, he was worried that his team would now be down three games to two in the Series. And in spite of his friendship with Roberto, there was no question that David wanted that World Series ring.

For the next several innings, the game went exactly as the former Rosemont Rocket power hitter had guessed. Neither team could get to the other's starting pitcher. The score remained 2-1, Dodgers, going into the sixth.

David stood in the on-deck circle watching his buddy pitch to Dwight Evert. He was amazed at the ease with which Roberto moved the ball from one location to the next, each with varying speed. Evert struck out on four pitches, never making contact with the ball.

As he stood in at the plate, David thought, *It's pretty much up to me. I've gotta have the best chance of figuring him out!*

He looked out at his old teammate and couldn't believe what he saw. It was as if Roberto was in another world. Their eyes met, but Magic looked right through him. He seemed to have total concentration.

Before he knew what was happening, DT saw the first pitch streak by him for a strike. Realizing that he had better crank up his own concentration level, he stepped out of the box. He walked back to the on-deck circle and grabbed a pine-tar rag.

Frankie Statler pulled him down so he could whisper in his ear. "Hey, Green. I've been watching this kid carefully. Every time he gets that first-pitch fastball by someone for a strike, he comes back and tries to get a strike with his curve. Watch for the curve and nail it!"

David thought back for a second and then patted Statler on the helmet. "You got it! Thanks."

He carefully dug a good foothold in the box and assumed his stance. "Okay, Ramirez, just try and sneak one by me!" he said out loud.

Roberto's next pitch came in high, right down the middle of the plate. Expecting it to curve down and in on him, David set up and unloaded a tremendous swing.

The ball popped into Henderson's glove before David's bat was even half way around. It wouldn't have mattered if he had swung earlier. The plane of his swing was a good foot under the ball.

David turned and looked at Statler. Statler shrugged.

"0 and 2 . . . great. Just where I wanna be," grumbled David as he tried to gather himself for the next pitch. "Who knows what the next one is gonna do."

He knew he was in the worst possible situation. A batter with no idea what the pitcher was going to throw next.

Choking up on his bat, David's only thought now was to protect the plate and try to get a piece of whatever was thrown. He didn't want the embarrassment of striking out.

He watched Roberto wind-up and throw. Frantically he tried to pick up the rotation of the ball to get some clue about what was coming.

Split-fingered fastball . . . outside corner, his mind's eye told him. His instinct paid off with a solid drive toward third. He sprinted out of the box toward first without even looking in the direction of his hit.

Ron Feffer, the Dodger third baseman, made a frantic dive for the ball. The line shot went just out of his reach, curving down the base line toward left field.

Looking over his shoulder briefly, David rounded first without hesitation and tore off toward second. The Dodger left fielder and shortstop were in furious pursuit of the hit. But before they could retrieve it and whip it back into the infield, David stood on second with a double.

The TV and radio announcers up in the booth were trying to explain how the ball must have had eyes to find the hole between Feffer and the bag. They also mentioned it was the greatest piece of two-strike hitting they'd ever seen.

"That David Green, 'DT' to his hometown fans, is some piece of work," they said.

Pulling his batting glove off as he stood on second, David had to smile to himself. He knew he'd been lucky. But he had an old saying in high school and the words came back to him now: "It's better to be lucky than good!"

He half expected Roberto to turn toward him and acknowledge him in some way, but no such luck. His friend continued to focus on his task.

With one out, David was still not convinced his hit had done much good. The other men in the line up didn't stand much of a chance against Ramirez in high gear.

As he edged off the bag to take his lead, he suddenly decided to try and make something happen on his own. Breaking with the pitch, he tried a daring steal of third base.

Caught off guard, Roberto's delivery to the plate was not quick enough to make up for the big jump David had gotten. The Boston center fielder slid under Henderson's throw and was safe by a foot.

"Wayda go, kid," his third base coach, Lou Winston, said. "Heads up play."

Nodding, David kept his eyes on Roberto. He was still waiting for some sign from his pal.

"Now you can score on any hit or a fielder's choice," Winston reminded him. "And be sure to tag up on a fly ball. We've gotta get you in somehow."

"Right," David answered blankly.

The next pitch to Statler was a crusher. It was a one-hopper right back to the mound. David had taken a couple of steps toward home but was able to stop himself in time. He hustled back to third and watched helplessly as Statler was gunned down at first.

Now there were two outs. The sacrifice fly or fielder's choice wouldn't score him anymore. Prospects were bleak for the Sox once again.

Rick Waldman, the Boston catcher stepped up to the plate. David knew that Rick was only batting .107 for the play-offs and World Series. He'd been in a bad slump. David figured that Rick's batting problems weren't going to be solved hitting against Magic.

Maybe I should go for home, he thought as he stood on the third-base bag.

He shook his head and discarded the idea. *Magic's delivery was too fast to make a move on.*

But as he was mentally talking himself out of the plan, he found himself running down the base line bluffing the steal. Henderson caught the Boston base runner out of the corner of his eye and rose up out of his crouch. David stopped and started backpedaling toward third. With one eye on David and one eye on the ball, Henderson goofed.

Roberto's pitch hit the edge of the oversized catcher's mitt and bounded away from Henderson toward the backstop. Seeing an opening, David grabbed it.

Racing toward home as fast as he could run, David watched the scene unfold in front of him. Henderson reached the ball quickly and scooped it up. Charging in from the mound, Roberto's job was to cover home plate.

David, Roberto and the throw from Henderson all reached the same spot at the same time. The collision was scary.

The players went down in a heap.

The home-plate umpire tried as best he could to sort out what happened. As the dust cleared, he could see David's foot still lying across the plate. Roberto struggled to get up, the ball cradled in his glove. In his judgement, there was only one call to make.

" *Safe!*" Wendelson shrieked.

Lasorda was out of the dugout in a blink of an eye. Charging the umpire, he was yelling, frustrated by the tieing run. But nothing was going to change the call. The score was now 2-2.

David ran back to the dugout. He watched Roberto carefully to see how he would react, but nothing seemed to bother him. Without breaking stride, he fanned Waldman on the next three pitches.

The Dodgers failed to retaliate in their half of the sixth so the score remained all tied up at two.

Boston's Mark Lawrence managed to get around on one of Roberto's fastballs in the eighth and send it deep toward center field. If the ball had been pulled a little bit, it might have had a chance to get out. But it turned out to be just another long out to end the inning. L.A.'s hitters still mounted no threat, so going to the top of the ninth, David felt his team was in a position to win. He got on deck, determined to break the tie.

The crowd was cheering on every pitch now, the importance of each out magnified by the lateness of the game. Ramirez had energy to burn. He fanned Dwight Evert, for the third time, on three pitches.

David tossed down his weighted bat and grabbed his regular stick. He walked slowly toward the box, planning his strategy and preparing himself mentally.

He dug in at the plate, one foot scratching out a hole . . . then the next. By the time he looked out to the mound, his mind was focused on one thing. The fact it was his long-time friend out there pitching no longer even registered in his mind.

He watched Roberto going into his windup and tried to focus on the white, horse-hide sphere in his hand. He wanted to start tracking it as soon as it rolled off the pitcher's fingertips.

Cocking his bat and starting his stride, David held up at the last instant and let the ball go by.

"Strike one," the umpire hollered.

David nodded in agreement. He knew when he stopped his swing it was a strike. He also knew there wasn't much he would have been able to do with it.

Out of the corner of his eye, he could see the Dodger catcher, shifting around behind the plate. David knew he was edging toward the inside corner which meant only one thing: an inside pitch.

Shifting his front foot slightly to the right, he opened up his stance to give himself more room to clear his hips. Shaving even a split second off the time of his swing might mean the difference.

The next pitch came in just as David suspected. It was right on the inside corner of the plate but moving slightly in on him. David again decided to lay off of it.

This time the call was a ball.

Roberto played with Green for two more pitches, one of them outside and one of them inside. Roberto got a call on one of them, David got the call on the other. The count stood at two balls and two strikes.

"Strike the bum out!" a fan screamed from behind the third base dugout. "He ain't nothing!"

His voice had risen so clear and loud over the other crowd noise that everyone in the infield area heard it. David watched as a smile crossed Roberto's lips. It was the first sign he'd seen of the old Magic.

David thought his patience had been rewarded when he watched the next pitch come streaming in. Thigh high, just on the inside half of the middle, it looked like a pitch that was made to order for him.

He started his powerful stride into the ball, ready to smash it on a long ride. At the last moment, he saw his mistake.

The ball started sinking. Trying desperately to adjust the swing he started, David lowered his shoulders and tried to golf the ball. The fat end of his bat just managed to catch the pitch.

The Dodger Stadium crowd froze for an instant. The ball jumped off David's bat and headed for the right-field wall. It was a long, high blast that had home-run written all over it.

David took a couple of steps toward first as he watched the flight of the ball. He stole a glance toward Roberto to catch his reaction too. Everyone in the park turned all their attention on the long fly ball.

As he approached first, David realized the ball was too high in the sky and the right fielder was still circling as if he was going to make the catch.

The crowd caught on to that fact also. In spite of the impressiveness of the blast, David realized that it wasn't going to make it. He'd gotten under the pitch slightly and most of the force had lifted, rather than driven, the ball.

When it finally settled down, it came to rest in the glove of the Dodger right fielder.

The L.A. crowd exploded in joy.

Roberto wiped a bead of perspiration from his forehead and breathed a sigh of relief.

David turned and headed for the Boston dugout, convinced in his mind that his team was doomed. When Frankie Statler bounced out to the first baseman to end the Red Sox ninth, it didn't look good for the visitors.

As he ran out to center field for the bottom of the ninth, all he could do was hope the Sox pitchers could keep the door closed on the Dodgers until his team could somehow get their offense in gear again. When Marty Barnett started the Dodgers off by striking out, David thought they might do it. Sneed had pitched a great game. Since that early uprising when L.A. got their two runs, he had shut them down on two hits.

It didn't even concern David when the next batter, Mike Lambert, walked. He was one of the only L.A. players who wasn't a threat to steal a base.

David kicked himself for not thinking of the obvious. It was the bottom of the ninth and they only needed one run. Lasorda didn't hesitate to pull Lambert and insert a pinch runner. Suddenly everything in the game was headed for a Dodgers win.

Pinch runner, Tyler Warne, had blazing speed. Knowing full well what the plan was, Sneed had a problem worrying about keeping him close to the base. As Warne danced off the bag and bluffed toward second, a game of catch between Reed and his first baseman went into effect.

David paced around in a circle out in center. "Just throw the ball," he called in frustration.

After seven throws to first, Sneed finally had to deliver to the plate. As soon as his leg moved toward home, Warne was off. Despite a perfect throw by Waldman, he was in easily for the stolen base at second.

"Damn!" yelled David. He felt the acid chewing away at his stomach.

Sneed turned his full attention to the next batter, Ron Feffer. Known as a clutch hitter, the Dodger team captain had a gleam in his eye. A runner in scoring position, the game on the line, everything was just the way he wanted.

Sneed came in with a fastball, just in case Warne took off again. Feffer's eyes lit up and he ripped the ball into center field.

David came charging in on the two hopper and gloved the ball cleanly. Warne had already hit the third-base bag and was digging for home.

Unleashing everything he had, David whipped the ball at the catcher.

Warne hit the dirt with his slide.

The throw was absolutely perfect. Waldman gloved the throw on one hop and turned to tag the Dodger runner. When he looked down, he couldn't believe his eyes.

Warne was already touching the plate with his foot. *Safe!*" screamed the umpire into the cheers of the crowd. It was the wave of his hands that told the story. No one could have heard him.

The Dodgers came pouring out of the dugout to congratulate Warne and Feffer. The fans tried to jump the barriers and join their heroes out on the field. Security guards did their best to stop them, but finally gave up.

David turned and ran toward the Boston exit and the safe confines of their clubhouse. He slammed his glove into the cubicle when he reached it and buried his head in his hands.

"We blew it!" he spat out. "I should have had him!"

Manager Joe Morgan heard his rookie and slapped him on the shoulder.

"Don't blame yourself, Green. Your throw was perfect. He just beat it."

"But coach . . . we're down 3-2."

Morgan ruffled his hair with his hand. "Hey . . . look at the bright side. We're going back home."

David reluctantly nodded.

Morgan smiled. "You've gotta remember the immortal words of Yogi Berra."

David looked at him again puzzled. "What?"

As he walked away toward his own locker, Morgan said, "It ain't over till it's over!"

TEN

Roberto stared out his airplane window into the bright, blue sky of a flawless October day. Just coming into view on the horizon was the city of Boston. The clearness of the autumn air allowed a breathtaking view of the old city.

Fresh off a victory in game five the night before, Roberto and his Dodger teammates were excited about coming back to Beantown. They knew they only had to win one more game. The pressure was on Boston.

It had been a tremendous series for the Dodger rookie. Winner of games two and five, with brilliant pitching performances in both, he stood a chance at series MVP if his team won. Two complete games, two victories and twenty strikeouts were impressive numbers to put up.

David had gotten a few hits off of him but, Roberto had done the important thing: he hadn't let DT's bat win any games for Boston.

After the day-long flight out from the West
Coast, the Dodgers fought their way through
rush-hour traffic and checked into their hotel. It
was too late to work out at the park, so Lasorda
had given them the night off. Regular curfew
hours were in effect, but the players were free to
do what they wanted.

A lot of guys chose to crash in their hotel rooms
and rest. Movies were on several player's minds.
Roberto was expecting visitors.

He plopped down on his bed and propped some
pillows up against the headboard. He positioned
the phone next to him and then flicked on the TV.
It wasn't long before the phone rang.

"Get your butt up and come on down here," the
voice on the other end yelled.

Roberto recognized Scrapper's voice immediately.

"What makes you so miserable?' Magic
laughed into the phone.

"Having to drive through town with Green,
that's what!" Glen said.

"Bad mood?"

"Listen . . . I'm not gonna sit here on a phone in
the lobby and explain it to you. Come on down
here and you can see for yourself." Scrapper hung
up.

When he reached the lobby, Roberto immediately spotted David ragging on Glen as they stood
by the house phone. It appeared Glen wasn't even
able to hang up before David was on him again.

"Hey, guys," Roberto waved. The smile on his face was a mile wide.

David came over and after smashing forearms with him, put his arm around Roberto's shoulders.

"Hey . . . take it easy on the shoulder, DT. It's still sore from banging into you last night."

David gripped him even tighter. "Great. At least I got one good lick in."

Roberto straightened up and shrugged David's arms off of him.

Glen broke in and pushed his buddies toward the door. "C'mon you jerks. Let's get outta here. I'm already tired of listening to the two of you."

They hit the cool, crisp evening air of Boston and walked around for awhile until they could hail a cab. They all jumped in and instructed the cabbie to head for Yaz's.

But, once inside the packed night spot, they resumed their bickering.

"I can't believe how lucky you guys have been," David complained.

"Lucky? What're you talking about? We've beaten you guys the same way we beat everyone all year . . . superior pitching and defense." Roberto sounded offended.

"Yeah, right. But talk about no offense. You guys couldn't hit your way out of . . . "

"Seems to me we've scored a few more runs than the team we're playing!"

"Flukes . . . every run you've gotten has been some flukey deal you didn't deserve."

Glen had to break in again. "Stop. I've heard enough. I'll settle this thing. Neither one of you're teams would exactly scare anybody right now with their hitting ability. But from where I've been sitting . . . it's been one heckuva series to watch. But I've got a complaint for both of you."

"Yeah, like what?" Green asked. "There's so much action, it's getting tougher and tougher to write my column."

David and Roberto looked at each other, took off their caps and started to beat Scrapper on the head. They all broke up laughing.

"And the other thing," Glen added. "is that the two of you have been unbelievable." Glen threw an arm around each of his friends. "And I'm proud of you."

"Let's get something in his stomach before he loses it totally." David said. "It's getting pretty deep don't ya think?"

Roberto agreed. "I can't figure out how to handle Mr. Nice Guy, here. I think I liked him better when he was always insulting us."

"That can be arranged, Ramirez," Glen said as he stuck a finger in Magic's chest.

"Waitress!" David whistled. "Emergency food for this table. Quickly."

After wolfing down steak sandwiches and two huge orders of fries the three former Rosemont Rockets started to return to normal.

"Okay guys," Glen said. "You've gotta give me some good lines or something to use in my story tomorrow. The writer has been on me to get some first-hand comments from the players. You guys are it."

Roberto and David looked at each other and winked. Neither one said a word.

"Did you hear me?" Glen asked. "I need you guys to say something smart."

Still silence from the two Series participants.

Glen caught on to the their game. "Tongue tied, I see. Oh well. I'll guess I'll just have to make up some quotes for the two of you and give you the credit for them. I'm sure I could come up with something *real* good."

"Wait a minute," came out of both of their mouths at once.

It was Glen's turn to laugh. "I knew that would bring you to your senses. So tell me. What's the word out of each locker room? How do the players feel about how the Series is going?"

"We're pretty happy," beamed Roberto. "Of course, being up three games to two helps. I'd say most of the guys are real loose . . . relaxed and ready I'd say."

"Well . . . it ain't gonna be easy," David cautioned. "We're not gonna lie down. You've gotta figure the next game is our last shot."

"Right on," Roberto said as he rose his fist in the air.

"But, if we win game six, the Series is all tied up, right?"

"Duh, let me get my calculator," Roberto groaned.

" . . . and then, it's a one-game series. And we're the ones playing at home."

Glen looked at David. After a long pause he nodded his head. "I can't argue with that."

Roberto took a long pull from his soda. "Guess we're all gonna have to wait till tomorrow."

Game Six started on a beautiful Saturday afternoon. The big guns were out for both teams. Their ace starting pitchers were gonna try and decide who lived and who died. It was Boston's Roger Cowans trying to keep his team alive, and Val Fernandez trying to nail the coffin shut on the Sox for the Dodgers.

Fenway was jammed to the rafters, the fire marshall obviously having looked the other way for this important game. The loyal Boston fans knew it was do or die for their guys and every effort would be made to keep them going.

Both starters were on fire to begin the game. Cowans fanned two of the first three batters he faced. Fernandez came right back and did the same to Boston's starting three. It was David's pop out behind the first-base bag that prevented three strikeouts from being recorded by L.A.'s pitcher.

For the Boston faithful, the game took on an eerie similarity to the others. The lineup of power hitters just couldn't get untracked. There were few hits and no runs after five innings. Luckily for Boston, it was the same for the Dodgers.

In the top of the sixth, Corbin Reese caught one of Roger Cowans fastballs and drove it hard toward the Green Monster out in left. The ball caromed off the wall and got away from the Sox left fielder, O'Meara. Reese slid into second just before the throw for a double.

When Marty Barnett followed with a clean single past first, Reese ran home with the first run of the game.

"Damn!" cursed David as he stomped around in center field. "We've gotta stop them!"

But for the Sox it was more of a problem getting started than it was stopping their opponents. After averaging close to six runs a game during the last month of the regular season, they weren't used to worrying about a team having a 1-0 lead.

Cowans settled down and retired the side to contain the damage. Even though it was a small one, Boston was again faced with digging out of a hole.

The Boston manager, Joe Morgan, paced up and down the dugout in front of his troops. He was desperately trying to find the right way to motivate them.

"C'mon, men. Charge up out there. Go to the plate with some confidence. We can take this guy. Fernandez shouldn't be stopping us like this!"

They agreed with their coach, but when they walked back to the bench after each out, all they could do was shake their heads.

The Dodgers protected their 1-0 lead until the seventh. They then did the unthinkable. They extended it. A lead-off walk to Toby Harris paid dividends for the Dodgers when Ron Feffer drove a two-strike pitch toward the towering green wall. The Green Monster swallowed it up. The two-run homer made it 3-0, L.A.

When they came to the plate in the bottom of the seventh, each Boston player knew it was time. The fans had risen for the seventh inning stretch and remained standing as Jason Burke started things off.

"C'mon, Red Sox!" the cheers echoed.

The organist pumped up the crowd further and soon everyone was stomping their feet. The old stadium started creaking and groaning from the stress.

The call went up, " *Let's go Sox! Let's go Sox!*"

Burke took the first pitch thrown and drilled into right field for a single. The fans roared their approval.

"Wayda go, Burke," his teammates yelled. "Now we're moving!"

Randy Bell strode to the plate next. Down by three, no one expected him to sacrifice. Boston needed a big inning and every one sensed this better be it.

David watched from the on-deck circle as Fernandez went into his stretch.

"C'mon, Randy . . . you can do it!" he pleaded.

Bell killed the first pitch through the hole between shortstop and second. For an anxious split-second, everyone watched as the Dodger shortstop scrambled and dove for the ball. But he couldn't get there in time and Bell's hit went on through for another single.

Now the crowd really exploded. Two men were on and David Green was coming to the plate. Everyone went nuts, chanting "DT . . . DT . . . DT" pleading for their power-hitting rookie to knock one "downtown."

Digging in deep with the cleats, David could feel the adrenaline pumping through his body. The fans' cheers echoed in his ears. He looked out at Fernandez, saw the worry on the pitcher's face, and knew he was his.

"C'mon, pal. Give me something to hit," David whispered under his breath.

But Tommy Lasorda was nobody's fool. He saw the same thing David did and quickly called time. He ran out to the mound and, after a brief discussion with Fernandez and Henderson, his hand went up toward the bullpen. He knew it was time to make a change.

"Damn," moaned David as he stepped out of the box and went back to the on-deck circle. He touched up his bat with the pine-tar rag and talked to Frankie Statler.

"Why'd they have to make the change now," grumbled David.

The question didn't need an answer. He knew it was to break up the Red Sox momentum and to bring in a fresh, strong arm.

"Don't worry about it, DT," Statler told him. "It doesn't matter who's up there now. We're on a roll."

"I hope you're right," David nodded as he walked back toward the plate.

Lasorda had called on Eric Knox to slam the door shut before it was too late. Knox had a 2.01 ERA for the season and had been the Dodgers' most consistent reliever. Having made appearances in sixty-five games, he wasn't going to rattle easily.

On his first pitch, David swung so hard he almost screwed himself into the ground for a strike.

"Settle down, Green," Morgan called from the dugout. "Stay in control." David shook his head sheepishly. He knew he'd looked stupid.

"I won't let that happen again," David promised.

True to his word, he was ready for the next pitch. Knox tried to sneak a curve ball by him on the outside corner. It hung a little too high. David jumped all over the pitch and hit a line shot to left.

The ball was on the wall before the Dodger left fielder could turn around. Burke scored easily from second and Bell legged it into third when the ball was late coming back to the infield.

There was no stopping the Sox and their fans now. Fenway park was rocking and rolling with the cheers and chants of the crowd.

Statler followed David's hit with another single, this one to right field. It drove in another run and David made it to third.

The momentum for the Sox was now like a steam roller. Anything in their path was going to get flattened. After a frustrating Series at the plate, the Boston batters had come alive.

Before the inning was over, Mark Lawrence ripped a double to center to score the tying and go-ahead runs. Dwight Evert and Rick Waldman both singled. And as icing on the cake, Jason Burke, who led off the inning, topped things off with a three-run homer. When the tally of damages was done, the score stood 8-3 for Boston.

When Cowans struck out the final Dodger batter in the ninth, the Fenway crowd went into a wild celebration. The series was now tied up three games apiece.

David ran through the tunnel from the dugout to the clubhouse with his fist in the air. "We did it . . . we did it! All right . . . one more to go!"

His cry echoed through the concrete walkway and was repeated by his teammates. The team started celebrating like it was the final game.

Morgan tried to gather his troops for a minute amidst the bedlam. Reporters and television cameras were already scrambling for interviews.

"Interviews can wait," he screamed out. "Everybody outta here for a second."

The tone of his voice led everyone quickly out.

He got his players around him and locked the clubhouse doors. He looked at all of them and said, "Okay, guys. You've taken the first step. The Dodgers had us down . . . but we came back!"

"Right on!"

"We're the best!"

"No one can keep us down, Coach!" the voices called out.

Morgan smiled. "That's right. And don't forget it. But we've still got the second step to take. All right, men. We're on a roll now. Let's do it!"

The clubhouse shook from the force of their cheers.

ELEVEN

Roberto woke up Sunday morning in his Boston hotel room after a horrible night's sleep. He and the whole team had taken the loss to the Red Sox hard. It was a game they all felt shouldn't have gotten away from them.

Sitting with a 3-0 lead, the World Championship had been only nine outs away. Now, it was going to go down to the seventh and deciding game.

The Dodgers were going to go with Terry Fulton out on the mound. They knew they'd probably face, Mike Harrisman, Boston's junk ball specialist. It was hard to predict who had the advantage there. But everyone knew momentum had switched to the Red Sox.

Roberto struggled out of bed and walked to the window to throw open the curtains. His roommate on the road, Marty Barnett, was still asleep. When he flipped open the heavily padded window coverings, he blinked from the light, then stood back in amazement.

"Holy smoke! . . . Where did this come from?" he moaned.

Barnett rolled over on the bed and tried to pull his pillow around his ears.

Roberto squinted and looked more closely outside. The sky was a heavy overcast and rain was pelting down against the window.

"Barnett . . . look at this," Roberto called out.

"Go away, Ramirez. It's too early."

"No . . . it's too late," Magic said.

Barnett rose up on one elbow and blinked the sleep out of his eyes. "What's the problem?"

"Rain. It's coming down pretty hard. I wonder if we're gonna get to play today."

"Probably just a shower," the veteran said. "It'll be fine by game time."

"Maybe," Roberto shrugged. The solid overcast sky made him doubt that.

By the time the two Dodger teammates got dressed, the sky looked even darker. When they joined the rest of their teammates for breakfast in the hotel dining room, everyone was concerned about the playing conditions.

They boarded their charter bus and rode to the ball park in relative silence. Everyone was still bummed out about the last game. After dropping their bags off in the clubhouse, most of the players wandered inside the stadium to check out the playing field. They saw that the ground crew had already covered the infield with a tarp.

"Doesn't look real good," Lasorda grumbled to no one in particular. "But . . . maybe that's not all bad."

His players looked at him and wondered what he meant.

They returned to the visiting team's locker room and prepared for the game as if it was on schedule. When it came time for batting practice though, they got the word that there wouldn't be any time for practice. The tarp was going to stay on the field right up till game time.

"Great," Ron Feffer grumbled. "They're gonna make us play this thing without any warm-ups. I sure as hell don't like that!"

Coach Westrum cut off the grumbling before it got out of hand. "It's the same story for both teams so just suck it up and forget it. Don't start beating yourself before you get on the field."

The players settled down and went about the usual pre-game rituals. The card players did their thing. The readers did theirs. The injured players got taped and wrapped and the nervous players paced around. Finally, it came time to go to the dugouts and the pregame introductions.

When they arrived in their dugout, they saw the team of umpires gathered around out at home plate. Lasorda jogged out to join them. Pulling up the zipper of his royal blue warmup jacket, he tucked his neck down in the collar to avoid the falling rain.

"This is ridiculous," Feffer complained as all the Dodgers stood huddled together watching the meeting out on the field.

"They can't make us play in this slop can they?" someone asked out loud.

"If the TV network has their way, we'll probably have to play. The only thing they're concerned about is beer ads." Everyone stood at the bottom step of the dugout, just under the edge of the protective eave, waiting for some sign from their coach. When he finally turned away from the umpires, he gave the thumbs down sign and waved his players back.

"We're outta here," he said as he hit the top step. "They called it?" Feffer asked. "Or are we just postponed till it stops?"

"It's called. They figure even if it stopped raining right now, the field is such a mess they couldn't get it fixed up in time. Besides, the radar reports from the weather station say this isn't going to let up for four or five more hours. We're done for the day."

There was a mixture of anguish and relief among the players. Some would have just as soon decided the Series one way or another right then and there. Others were glad they had another day to get their spirit back.

As they changed back out of their uniforms and headed for the bus, the players were pretty sub-

dued. For some reason Lasorda seemed almost
happy.

Monday morning dawned clear and bright. The
air was fresh from the cleansing rain, and Boston
was alive again with sunshine and blue skies.
The day off had done a world of good. The players
had driven the disappointing loss in game six
from their minds and the return of the sun lifted
the gray gloom of the day before.

"This is great," said Roberto as he walked out
of the hotel.

Steve Henderson agreed. "Reminds me of Wyoming. A good thunderstorm would really clear
the air back home. Maybe that rain yesterday did
the same for us."

When they got to Fenway, the stands already
had a few fans filtering in, even though it was
still three hours till game time. A lot of the loyal
Boston fans, enjoyed watching batting practice
because of all the long ball activity.

"How long can they stomach sitting out in
those bleachers?" Roberto asked. "You'd think
they'd get pretty bored waiting."

Feffer grumbled, "They're like vultures out
there. Waiting for us to roll over."

"Too bad they're gonna be disappointed," said
Roberto. " Cause we're gonna win!"

"Right on!" Feffer said, high-fiving him.

After entering the locker room and sitting
down to suit up, Roberto heard his name yelled

from the corner of the room. He stood up and saw his manager waving him toward the office.

"Ramirez," Lasorda called out. "I wanna talk to you." Roberto finished buttoning his shirt as he walked the short distance to Lasorda's office. He entered and sat down across the desk from his coach.

"Ramirez," Lasorda addressed him as he watched him carefully. "You up to pitching today?"

Roberto almost fell backward in his chair.

"What . . . but . . . I thought . . . " he stammered.

"Arm okay?"

"Sure."

Lasorda stood up from his chair. "I know I didn't say anything to you yesterday, 'cause I wasn't sure until this morning. You've had three days off since game five. I know we usually throw everybody after four days rest. But hey, there is no tomorrow."

Roberto gulped. "I know."

Lasorda continued. "Ramirez . . . you've been the best we've got the past month. If it wasn't for you we wouldn't have won the NLCS. No one's been more effective against the Sox either. I'd just as soon take my chances with you today if you think you can go."

Roberto was lost in his own thoughts for a second. After he noticed a long silence he realized he was supposed to answer that last statement.

"Coach, I can do it," he declared. "I won't let you down."

"I know you won't, kid," the manager nodded. He patted Roberto on the back and said, "Finish getting ready and we'll go warm up. See how the arm's feeling."

Magic left the office in a daze. When he got back to his locker, Henderson walked over and sat down next to him.

"What's up, kid?" he asked.

"I'm throwing today."

"Great! I was hoping they'd figure that out."

Magic turned to look at his teammate. "You mean that?"

"Nah, I just need somebody to make me look good!"

Roberto smiled and grabbed his hat. "Okay, man . . . I'm ready!"

Despite making his third appearance in the Series, Roberto was still nervous as he took the mound in the first inning. His teammates had been retired in order in their half of the first and now it was up to him to keep the Sox bats under control.

"Settle down," he told himself over and over again. He could feel his heart beating in his throat.

After Roberto's warm-up tosses, Henderson pegged the ball down to second and then came out to the mound. He wanted one more talk with his pitcher to help get him primed.

"You ready, Magic man?" he asked.

"I guess so," Roberto answered, his eyes roaming the jam-packed stadium.

"Okay then, remember to stay loose and follow through. Use those legs to drive your body. Don't try to do to much, just let it all flow smoothly."

Roberto silently nodded.

"Okay, then let's win this sucker."

Roberto watched him trot back behind the plate. Jason Burke stepped into the box to lead off the game for Boston. When Magic looked in for the sign, Henderson was making all kinds of weird gestures with his fingers. Magic couldn't help smiling.

When Henderson saw his pitcher laughing, he gave the high sign and then signaled for a fastball.

Roberto threw a bullet right down the middle. Burke stood an watched as the ball zipped by him.

"Striiike one," sang the umpire.

A curve ball followed by another fastball, resulted in the first strikeout of the game for Roberto.

"Wayda fire, Magic . . . wayda fire!" his teammates cheered.

Lasorda flashed a thumbs up sign from the dugout. He liked what he saw to start the game.

Randy Bell and Dwight Evert followed Burke to the plate . . . and to the dugout. Roberto struck out the side to end the first inning.

"Whew," he gasped as he plopped down on the Dodger bench. "I'm glad that's over with it."

"The first inning is always the roughest, isn't it?" Henderson said. "Should be smooth sailing now, kid."

The Dodger catcher stood and walked up and down the bench, nervously pacing off excess energy.

Boston's starter, Mike Harrisman walked Corbin Reese to start the second inning. The Dodger bench came alive, trying to get a rally going. When Marty Barnett followed with a single, everyone was on their feet standing on the steps of the dugout cheering.

"Let's go, guys . . . let's go!" Lasorda clapped.

Knowing Roberto would keep the score down, Lasorda flashed the sacrifice sign to the third base coach. He in turn, relayed it to the batter, Mike Lambert. When Harrisman started his delivery, Lambert squared around to bunt.

The Boston third and first basemen came charging hard toward the plate. The second baseman covered first and the shortstop moved toward third. Everyone worked in perfect unison.

Lambert's bunt forced the third baseman to field it. Lawrence had no other play but first and the two Dodger runners advanced.

"Nice job, Mike. Good bunt." Everyone congratulated him on the sacrifice.

Everything worked like clockwork when the next batter, Ron Feffer, laced a single to right and both Reese and Barnett scored. The Dodger bench and the few fans they had up in the stands went nuts. Things looked very good for the Dodgers.

Harrisman bore down though and got the next batter, Toby Harris, to bounce into a double play to end the inning. But it was a charged up Dodger ball club that took the field in the bottom of the second. They had a 2-0 lead . . . and Magic on the mound.

TWELVE

David Green stepped up to the plate to lead off the second inning. Disgusted that his team had fallen behind, he knew he'd better get something going before his old teammate reached full strength.

Holding up his right hand for time, David made an extra effort to dig into the ground in the batter's box and get a good foot hold. He slammed the bat down hard on the edge of the plate and then stared out at his high school buddy. He could see Roberto focused in on his catcher's target.

Roberto started his windup and came in with his fastball. It was a blur to the people in the stands. No one in the field could really follow its flight. But David was ready.

He released the coiled spring tension in his shoulders and started the bat on a lightning fast trip of its own. The two speeding objects came together over the plate in a frightening collision.

The strength behind David's swing overcame the momentum of Roberto's pitch. The ball ricocheted off his bat and jetted out toward right field. No one in the Dodger outfield even moved.

David watched the flight of the ball for a split second and then slammed his bat down on the ground. He started into his home-run trot and raised one fist in the air.

The ball rose up over the roof in right field and disappeared into some Boston neighborhood, two blocks away. Stunned for a moment, the crowd finally erupted into cheers. As he circled the bases, David kept his head down and avoided looking at Magic.

When he touched the plate, he was mobbed by teammates. Everyone was talking about the unbelievable length of the blast.

Up in the press box, Glen Mitchell heard one of the radio announcers tell his listeners, "Ladies and Gentleman, that ball would have been out of any park in the country . . . and that includes Yellowstone National Park!"

Glen had to nod his head in silent agreement.

The fans continued screaming and cheering after David disappeared into the dugout. Fenway Park had gone completely bonkers.

"Green," Morgan yelled. "You'd better get back out there and tip your hat or something. They'll tear off the roof of this place if you don't."

Embarrassed, David didn't know what to do. His teammates literally pushed him back out toward the field.

Finally, David stepped out from under the cover of the dugout for a curtain call. He lifted his hat off of his head and waved it to the crowd. They screamed their heads off and continued applauding after he jumped back inside.

Despite the uproar and wild celebration, one fact remained unchanged. The Red Sox were still behind. David's blast had only narrowed the score to 2-1. But it had put spirit back into his team.

The two pitchers again gained control of the game. Roberto immediately settled down and retired the next nine men in a row. Harrisman had little trouble during that stretch with the Dodgers. Going into the bottom of the fifth, the score remained the same.

When David stepped up to the plate to face his former Rosemont teammate again in the fifth, the crowd came back to life.

He again dug in a firm foothold and got ready for Roberto's pitch. Much to everyone's surprise, Roberto again challenged him.

The fastball came zipping in with everything he could put on it. David ripped his bat at the ball, but this time came up empty.

"Strike one!" the umpired bellowed out.

David kicked at the dirt around the white chalk line of the box. *Damn . . . I should have had that one*, he thought.

Roberto came in with a screwball. David wisely layed off of it as it broke down and away from him. But, the umpire saw the pitch differently and called it another strike.

In the hole against Magic was not where he wanted to be. When the next pitch came streaking in, David hesitated for a split second, not sure if it was a waste pitch or not. When it broke down across the plate, it was too late for him to react.

"Strike three . . . you're outta there!" was the call.

As he walked back to the dugout, David heard the Dodgers cheering their teammate on. *Game's not over yet*, he thought to himself as he slammed his bat back in the rack.

The game continued for two more innings with the score remaining, 2-1 for L.A. In the top of the seventh, the Dodgers were feeling very good.

Salazar, started things off for L.A. in the seventh by rapping a double into the left-field corner. The throw into second was close but he got the call in his favor. His teammates were up and cheering immediately.

"Thata way, man . . . let's get some insurance!"

"It's just the start!"

When Reese followed with an infield single, things were really looking up. Salazar made it to third, so L.A. had runners on the corner with nobody out.

Boston's manager Joe Morgan went to the mound. After talking with Waldman, the Sox catcher, he decided to make a move. He waved his left hand to bring in Frank Washington.

While the reliever warmed up out on the mound, Roberto paced the Dodger dugout. Although he was pitching masterfully, he needed some more runs as backup. Just in case there was another slip like the one to David.

"C'mon guys . . . let's keep it going," he hollered out.

Washington was very tentative against the first batter he faced. So tentative that he wound up walking Mike Lambert. Now the bases were loaded.

With Ron Feffer at the plate, the Dodger captain, and a definite long ball threat, the Boston crowd was quietly sitting on the edge of their seats. They knew the next few minutes could be the game.

Washington, working from the stretch, started his wind-up. In the blink of an eye, he fired the ball to first. Caught completely off guard, Lambert was four steps off the bag and leaning toward second. Before he knew what hit him, he was picked off.

The crowd roared their approval and were back in the game, cheering loudly. That one play had stopped the Dodger momentum cold.

Washington struck out Feffer. The very first pitch to Wells was hit back meekly to the first baseman who just stepped on the bag for the final out. The big Dodger rally fizzled. Roberto had no insurance.

David stood in the on-deck circle in the bottom of the seventh. Thankful his team had dodged a bullet in the top half of the inning, he was still worried about their offense. Magic had mowed his teammates down in every inning and he knew that the end was near. It looked grim.

When the first batter quickly popped out behind the plate, David strode to the box with one thought in mind: home run.

The crowd's chanting was at a fevered pitch. They wanted the same thing David did.

Green watched as Roberto took a deep breath and wiped the sweat from his brow. He went into his windup and delivered.

In a flash, David spun and fell to the ground. Roberto's pitch had risen, hard and fast, right toward David's head.

The Boston bench was immediately on its feet and ready to head for the field. He yelled at his teammates, "Stop . . . stop. Forget it!"

"Sit down, everybody," Morgan shouted. "Let Green handle this." Morgan was trying to rein in his players also. The last thing he wanted was a brawl.

David quickly scrambled up and held his hand in the air. "I'm okay," he yelled out loud. He looked out toward his friend on the mound.

Roberto shrugged apologetically, stepped off the mound and headed for the rosin bag. It was his way of saying that the ball had slipped. Trying to put everything he could into the pitch, he'd let it get away from him.

Henderson could see his pitcher was upset. He ran out to the mound to talk to him.

"Hey, man . . . I know this guy's your friend. Don't let it bother you. Things happen."

Roberto whipped around and faced his catcher. "I could've killed him! I can't believe I could even throw something that bad!"

"C'mon . . . it just slipped. No big deal . . . he got outta the way . . . no problem."

Roberto's mind's eye quickly flashed on a young Billy Mills, sprawled in the dirt with blood coming out of his ear. That near tragedy in Albuquerque had almost cost Roberto his career. He felt his nerves tighten and his breathing became more labored.

Henderson could see the emotion welling up in his pitcher's eyes. "Don't you chump out on me, kid. This is the seventh game of the World Series here. Half the world is watching this game. And it's a good bet, half of those people are pulling for us to win. You owe them, the rest of the guys on the team, me and most of all yourself, to give it the best you've got." Roberto looked into Henderson's eyes. He tried to blink back the tears in his own. For a moment, neither player said a word.

Finally, with a deep breath, Magic took the ball out of Henderson's glove and pointed him toward the plate. Henderson turned to walk back.

David had watched the scene out on the mound and knew his buddy was in trouble. He was torn between sympathizing for him and his own desire to win. When it appeared Magic was ready to pitch again, all doubt was wiped from his mind.

"Just put one over the plate," he mumbled as he took his stance.

The very next pitch was a screamer that hit the outside corner. Seeing that he couldn't use it, David let it go. The umpire called it a strike.

After a curveball, low and away, he watched as another fastball headed toward him. This one was going to catch the inside corner, so he decided he'd better go for it. His bat just caught a piece of it, the ball sinking suddenly as it crossed the plate. It bounded foul behind the catcher.

"Great," muttered David. "Now I'm down 2-2." He choked up on the bat and edged forward in the box.

David stood handcuffed when the next pitch came across the plate. It was the best curveball he'd ever seen. As he was walking back to the dugout after the strikeout, he was still marveling at the pitch.

Morgan met him at the dugout steps. "Did that pitch move as much as it looked like from here?" he asked in amazement.

"Coach, no way anybody could hit that."

Frankie Statler then struck out to end the seventh.

Washington did his job again in the eighth with a quick one-two-three inning. Boston came right back up to the plate, now with only six outs remaining.

David had been the only Boston hitter to even touch Roberto. When he was retired in the seventh, it looked like it would be clear sailing for Magic the rest of the way.

Mark Lawrence stepped into the box to lead off the eighth for the Red Sox. Seemingly in complete command, Roberto rifled a fastball on the outside corner. The switch-hitting Lawrence leaned across the plate and slapped at the pitch. He got under it and it flew out toward left field. It looked like a routine fly ball, but then the unexpected happened. The left fielder kept drifting back, pounding his glove, ready to make the catch. The lazy fly just kept floating. Suddenly, without any warning, it was gone.

The short fence in left field, the fabled Green Monster, had swallowed it up.

The Boston crowd went berserk. Everyone was on their feet screaming and cheering. The score was now knotted at two up.

David watched Roberto standing on the mound. He kept staring out at the fence in disbelief.

Roberto gathered himself quickly and retired the side after that. The two teams were headed to the ninth all tied up, 2-2.

The Dodgers were three up and three down in the their half of the inning. The Boston crowd could taste victory.

But Roberto was not to be denied. Three Boston batters came up and three went down, two by strikeouts. The regulation nine innings were over. They were headed for extra innings.

As David ran out in the field to start the tenth, he jogged with Mark O'Meara. The veteran left fielder turned to David and said, "It doesn't get any better than this, does it, kid?"

"Pretty unbelievable," David said. "I don't know how this game's gonna turn out."

"Who does?" laughed O'Meara as he veered off toward his position.

The Dodgers had been unable to touch Boston's Washington. But Feffer started off the inning with a walk. When he was successfully sacrificed to second, the Dodger bench came alive with cheers.

Henderson came to the plate. Washington worked him carefully and ran the count to three balls and two strikes. The Boston crowd was on pins and needles. The tension was mounting on every pitch.

"Don't walk him," David yelled out. "Make him be a hitter."

Washington thought the same thing. He came in with a strike for the last pitch. Henderson was waiting.

The Dodger catcher took the pitch and drove it on a line over the shortstop's head and into the gap between left and center. By the time David got to it, there was no play at home. The Dodgers had grabbed the lead again.

Morgan went to the mound and brought in a reliever. Henderson had made it to second to get into scoring position. The Boston players knew they had to stop that run from scoring.

Tony Leonetti came in for Sox to pitch. He immediately struck out Marshfield and Salazar to end the inning. It was all coming down to the end.

The first batter up in tenth was Randy Bell. On Roberto's first pitch, Bell drove a towering blast down the left-field line that bounced into the street beyond the ball park. It was foul by inches. The crowd groaned.

Tommy Lasorda immediately hopped up onto the first step of the dugout. He looked at the catcher. Henderson just shrugged.

When Roberto bounced the next two pitches into the dirt, Lasorda went to the mound.

"How's the arm, kid? You look like you're getting tired."

Magic threw his shoulders back and rolled his head around on his neck. "I think I'm okay, Coach."

Henderson spoke to the manager for his pitcher. "He's losing a little stuff on the fastball . . . but his breaking ball is still moving real well."

Lasorda was torn. He hesitated for a minute and then patted Magic on the back. "Keep it down, kid. Listen to what Henderson tells ya."

Roberto nodded.

Before he even settled back in the dugout, Lasorda watched the next pitch to Bell. It was long fly ball toward straight away center. Salazar raced back toward the wall. At the last possible instant, he jumped and made the catch.

Lasorda was back to the mound before the ball was back in the infield.

"That's it, kid . . . it's time!"

Roberto tried to put up an argument, but there was no choice now. It was the second trip to the mound and that was an automatic pull. The two of them walked back to the dugout together.

"You did a great job, Ramirez. The three days rest is just catching up with ya. Ten innings is a long way to go."

Roberto had to agree. As soon as he'd stepped off the mound, he realized how bone-tired he really was. Lasorda smiled at him. "Two more outs and you're a hero anyway. Let's sit down and see what happens."

Terry Fulton was out on the mound for the Dodgers now. His job was to get two outs. The Boston fans were pleading for something different.

When Dwight Evert stepped up to the plate, David came out of the dugout and got in the on-deck circle. He called out to his teammate, "Get something started, Dwight. We need you!"

Evert took the words to heart. He worked the count carefully to three and two by fouling off four pitches. He hung in there long enough that he finally got a base on balls.

David came to the plate and Fenway Park came unglued. Everyone was on their feet. Down 3-2, bottom of the tenth, with their best power hitter up, they were begging for deliverance.

"DT . . . DT . . . DT . . . " the crowd chanted.

David felt the goosebumps run up and down his spine. His heart was beating so fast that he stepped back from the plate for a minute to slow himself down.

As he looked around the park, the fans were waving, clapping and shouting. The noise was almost deafening. It was like nothing he could have ever imagined.

Fulton worked from the stretch. He checked the runner at first and then fired. David swung and smashed a one hopper right to his own first base coach. The foul ball put him down in the count, 0-1.

Fulton realized the runner wasn't going anywhere so he concentrated fully on David. He came
in with a beauty of a breaking ball that nipped
the inside corner. Quickly the count had fallen to
0-2.

David lifted his head up and exhaled slowly.
"Make it good, Green," he told himself.

Fulton toyed with the outside corner of the
plate on his next two pitches. They were off
enough that David wasn't concerned about a bad
call. He just let them go. The umpire agreed and
the count evened at 2-2.

Cocking his bat, David didn't even bother choking up. He only had one thing in mind right now:
Find a good pitch and drive it hard.

Fulton came down with his best — another
breaking ball that started high and inside. This
time David was ready. Fenway Park exploded at
the same time the bat crashed into the ball.
Catching it with every fiber of his body, the game
was over. In an instant of tremendous raw power,
David had snatched victory away from the Dodgers and handed it to the hometown Red Sox.

Hit on a line, the ball rose majestically into the
upper deck in right field. As the Dodgers wandered off the field in a state of shock, the Boston
fans raced to get on it. Security guards and police-
man fought a hopeless battle.

David had to pick his way through the crowd to
circle the bases. A thousand hands tried to slap
him and pat him on the back. His eyes filled with

tears as he approached home. He stole one quick glance toward the Dodger dugout.

Roberto stood alone leaning against the bat rack. He flashed a thumbs up sign to his friend.

When DT approached home plate, a path was cleared and he made a huge jump to touch the base. He was lifted on the shoulders of his teammates and carried around the field.

Fans were tearing up big chunks of sod from the field for souvenirs. Bedlam, mayhem and delirium were the only words to describe the scene.

The Public Address announcer shouted over and over again, "The *Boston Red Sox are Champions Of The World!*"

When the Sox finally reached the safe confines of their clubhouse, every player was sprayed with champagne as they walked in the door.

The television announcers were there with cameras and microphones stuck in everybody's face.

While Manager Joe Morgan was on the dais receiving the World Series trophy from the Commissioner of Baseball, David got called up in front to help hoist the huge award overhead. The whole team cheered as they passed it around for each player to enjoy.

The wild Red Sox celebration was interrupted for a moment. Tommy Lasorda and several of the Dodger players came into the Red Sox clubhouse. In the true spirit of sportsmanship, they offered their congratulations on the great Series win.

The party was in full swing, when David wiped his eyes of champagne with a towel.

When his vision cleared, he saw Glen and Roberto standing in front of him. After a crushing forearm smash for both of them, he threw his arms around them and hugged them.

"Helluva series, man . . . you deserved to win."

"Thanks, Magic. That means a lot to me."

Roberto hugged him again. "Losing to the best takes some of the sting off." He stepped back. "But wait till next year!"

"Hey," Glen shouted, "that my line!"

The three Rosemont stars laughed and raised their hands in the air for the highest high five of all time.

Football.
Basketball.
Baseball.

HEROES INC.

has the game for you.

Published by Ballantine Books.